Y0-EIK-076

Chi Chisholm, Matt
 Death trail
 Large Print

DATE DUE			
JUN 17 1999			
JUL 08 1999			
JUL 26 1999			
AUG 14 1999			
FEB 01			

DISCARD

Loogootee Public Library
410 N. Line St.
Loogootee, Ind. 47553

GAYLORD M2G

SPECIAL MESSAGE TO READERS

This book is published by
THE ULVERSCROFT FOUNDATION
a registered charity in the U.K., No. 264873

The Foundation was established in 1974 to provide funds to help towards research, diagnosis and treatment of eye diseases. Below are a few examples of contributions made by THE ULVERSCROFT FOUNDATION:

A new Children's Assessment Unit at Moorfield's Hospital, London.

•

Twin operating theatres at the Western Ophthalmic Hospital, London.

•

The Frederick Thorpe Ulverscroft Chair of Ophthalmology at the University of Leicester.

•

Eye Laser equipment to various eye hospitals.

If you would like to help further the work of the Foundation by making a donation or leaving a legacy, every contribution, no matter how small, is received with gratitude. Please write for details to:

**THE ULVERSCROFT FOUNDATION,
The Green, Bradgate Road, Anstey,
Leicester LE7 7FU. England
Telephone: (0533)364325**

DEATH TRAIL

McAllister rides again — against the cattle-kings of the high prairie ... He was alone in the darkness with enemies all around him. As a dark figure loomed up near him he lunged forward, raising his knife for the death thrust. When the man cried out the guns were turned on McAllister, and the lead whined about him, searching him out.

MATT CHISHOLM

DEATH TRAIL

Complete and Unabridged

LINFORD
Leicester

First published in Great Britain by
Panther Books Limited
London

First Linford Edition
published March 1992

Copyright © 1967 by P. C. Watts
All rights reserved

British Library CIP Data

Chisholm, Matt *1919* –
 Death trail.—Large print ed.—
 Linford western library
 I. Title
 823.914 [F]

ISBN 0–7089–7165–2

Published by
F. A. Thorpe (Publishing) Ltd.
Anstey, Leicestershire

Set by Words & Graphics Ltd.
Anstey, Leicestershire
Printed and bound in Great Britain by
T. J. Press (Padstow) Ltd., Padstow, Cornwall

1

THE night was calm and cold. There was no moon but there was a cloudless sky that was full of bright stars. The three men going slowly along the trail could see where they were going.

They were not tense, but they were excited as such men usually were when there was violence in the offing.

"How far?" Willy Toff asked, turning in the saddle. "Can't be far now?" He was the most eager of the three because he was the youngest and he had not been on such an expedition before. He kept thinking of the rope hanging from the right of his saddle and how within the hour the noose of it could be around the neck of a living man and strangling the life from him.

Charlie Strange said: "It ain't far." He was a dour man and nobody knew what he thought. He kept himself to himself and had no friends. He was hired to be here, so here he was. He would do this job without feeling as he did all the others.

The rear was brought up by Church, really their leader, for he was a range detective employed by the Hume Land and Cattle Company. Some said that he worked for the Cattlemen's Association. Whoever he worked for, everybody knew that he was a man best left alone. He had brought his reputation north with him from Arizona where he had scouted against Geronimo, showing great bravery, and where in one town or another he was said to have shot at least three men to death.

"Hold it," he called now with a slight sound of urgency in his voice.

"What?" Willy called.

"Pull off the trail. Somebody comin'."

They all halted and listened and heard the rider coming toward them from the north.

"Who the hell — ?" Willy wondered.

They walked their horses off the trail and Church said: "With luck it could be him. Anything not to have to mess with his wife and kids."

One of their horses whinnied and the animal coming along the trail gave an answering call. Church swore softly. The hoofbeats came nearer. Church opened his sheepskin coat so that his hand could reach the butt of his gun. As the oncoming rider loomed through the starlight, he urged his horse forward to meet him.

Church sang out: "Who's this?"

The rider came on, unsuspicious.

"Tom Holley," he called back. "Who's this?"

"Church."

The name stopped Holley as if he had ridden into a brick wall.

"What do you want?"

"We want you."

Strange and Toff walked their horses out of the brush into the starlight. Holley showed a little alarm and moved so suddenly in the saddle that his horse started acting up.

"Me? What do you want with me?" There was alarm in the man's voice. He knew them, he knew who they worked for and he knew the threats that had been made. He knew that Toff and Strange worked for Hardy Rigden. He recognized them in the dim light and he knew Rigden's reputation, the reputation that he had brought north two years ago from Texas. He had brought five thousand cows with him, too. Men like Tom Holley were said to live on Rigden beef. Rigden had been shouting that for a year in town, loud enough for the whole territory to hear. And, he said, if the Association didn't do something about it, he would. He would make an example and that wouldn't be forgotten for many a long year.

Church said: "Mr. Rigden said for you to stop it, Holley. He told you nice and civil. But you wouldn't listen."

"You ain't pinnin' no rustlin' on me."

"It's pinned."

"Not in no court of law. This is the sheriff's business."

"A nester's sheriff. Don't make me smile."

"You can't prove a thing."

"We don't have to prove anything. We know."

"Now see here — "

Willy, who had sidled his horse up to Holley, hit him around the mouth with the back of his hand. The nester gave a growl of rage and went to launch himself from the saddle at the little cowhand. Church drew his gun.

"Back up," he said. "Be still or I'll blow your fool head off."

"See if he has a gun on him, Willy."

With a little eager sound in his thin throat, Willy scrambled down from his horse, slapped his hands onto Holley and hauled him from the saddle. Scared the nester might be, but the sudden violence had snapped his frozen immobility. His work-hardened muscles snapped into action. He landed awkwardly on his feet, got himself foursquare on them and struck out at the small cowhand. The sound of his fist on the bony face reached the other two men. They saw Willy fall in a heap.

Holley stood over him and said: "Git up, you little bastard. I'll break your Gawd-damned neck."

There came the sound of Church cocking his gun.

"Back up," he said softly and there was no disobeying that voice.

Willy hauled himself to his feet, muttering: "I'll kill him."

Church said: "Search him, Willy. Just see he doesn't have a gun or a knife."

"I never carry a gun," Holley said almost proudly.

"More fool you," said Church.

Willy went up to the nester and tore his coat open. He ran his hands over the man's stout body and produced a short-bladed knife. He tossed this away into the darkness.

Church said: "Get on your horses an' we'll ride."

"Where you fellers takin' me?" Holley demanded in a voice that shook.

Willy laughed with the tremor of excitement in his voice.

"Where there's a tree that fits you," he said.

Holley fell back a pace.

"Wait a minute," he said. "You can't mean this. This is some sort of joke. Christ, I got a wife and kids."

They stayed still, watching him, almost able to smell his fear.

"Get on your horse," Church said.

"You can't make me. I ain't a-goin'."

Willy said: "Git on your horse, nester."

Holley started to go backward.

"No," he said. "No . . . no . . ."

He backed past Charlie Strange who leaned on his saddlehorn and watched him imperturbably. Suddenly, Holley gave Strange a quick look and turned and bolted.

It wasn't Church that fired, though he had a gun cocked in his hand. It was Strange. The silent man put his hand inside his coat, pulled out a long-barrelled Colt, cocked it without hurry and fired.

The horses all jumped a little at the sound of the shot and the bridle chains rattled their music.

The running man seemed to trip on his own feet. They heard the breath go out of him as he hit the ground. He cried out: "My Gawd, you've shot me," and clutched at his leg.

Church walked his horse up to him and said: "Now get on your horse or the next one'll be through your head."

"I can't stand."

The man started shaking with shock.

Little Willy ran at him and kicked him in the side.

"Git on yo' feet or I'll put the spur on you."

Holley looked slowly from one to the other of them, his face all twisted up and slowly rose to his feet. He tried to walk, but his right leg gave under him. He clutched it with both hands above the knee, making a groaning sound deep in his throat. Church kneed his horse forward, so that its shoulder nudged at the wounded man. Gradually, he was pushed forward, limping and groaning till he reached his horse. With a moan of agony, he put his injured foot in the stirrup-iron and heaved his injured leg over the cantle.

"Let me tie somethin' around my leg," he begged.

Willy giggled.

Holley whispered: "My Gawd, you fellers is Injuns."

Church said: "Lead on, Charlie."

Strange turned his horse and led the way off the trail. Holley was driven after him. Willy followed right behind him and Church brought up the rear. They headed east. It started to rain, at first lightly, but with a gradually growing weight. Soon they rode crouched forward in the saddle against it. Every now and then Holley turned in his saddle either angrily cursing them or beseeching them to let him go. He brought his wife and his kids into it several times, but he might as well have saved his breath. Women meant only one thing to these men and for them children did not exist. They rode for an hour before Strange halted. The rain had stopped and the prisoner saw that there were trees near. He looked at them in horror. He started to tremble violently; a small rivulet of spittle trickled down his chin.

Strange spoke.

"I'm cold and hungry. Let's git it over with quick."

The wind blew down from the hills and sang eerily through the trees. The spot was lonely enough for any deed. There would be no fear of discovery here.

Church said to Willy: "Throw your rope over a branch, Willy."

"My rope?" Willy said. "Why do we have to use my rope?"

"It's the only one we have."

Willy swore. It frightened him a little, knowing that the killing could be traced to him through the rope. But then he thought of Mr. Rigden and he knew he was safe. Rigden looked after his own. He reached forward and unfastened the rope from his saddle. Church indicated the tree he wanted used and Willy stood in his stirrups to make his throw. He was good with a rope and made it first time. He caught hold of the hanging noose with his hand and pulled it down, then he dismounted and fastened the end of the rope to the tree.

Holley sat his horse saying, "No ... no ... no ... " over and over. The three men dismounted and went and dragged his horse under the overhanging bough of the tree; they fastened his hands behind his back with pegging string and then they were all set.

"Christ!" Holley said, weeping now. "Don't you have no feelin' or mercy. I never did nothin' to you. All I did was claim land Rigden wanted. There's a law. You can't do this."

Church shouted: "Hold your noise."

But the man went on yelling and the sound of it jarred on the nerves of the three men.

Strange said: "Git that horse out from under, Willy."

Holley started shouting: "No . . . no . . . No . . . " again and tried to get out of the saddle.

Willy leaned from the saddle, quirt raised. He howled: "Aaaaah!" and lashed at the rump of Holley's horse with his quirt. The animal went still for a moment as it bunched its muscles under it, then it bounded forward. Holley seemed to be jerked violently out of the saddle. The scream that started from his throat was choked off. He kicked frantically for a short while. The three men sat their horses and stared as if frozen. Slowly the shock of the thing wore off a little. Church reached inside his coat for his gun. He raised it and fired three times at the now feebly jerking figure at the end of the rope.

All energy left it and it hung limply, swaying on the end of the rope.

Church said: "It's done. Let's get back."

They turned and rode south, sobered and chilled, each man occupied with his thoughts.

The woman came out of the sod-house at the sound of the shot. Behind her, through the open doorway followed the faint wail of a child.

"Tom," she called. "Tom, air you there?"

She was frightened. She had a face worn by work and want and now it was strained by worry. Both she and her husband had been on edge since Rigden had issued his warning a week back. Lon Freeman, his foreman, had ridden over and delivered it. He had ridden up to the house and told them to clear out. They were given two days to pack up and go. And they hadn't gone, because there was nowhere to go and Tom Holley had set his heart on making a go of things here. He was supposed to have rustled beef. Why they had picked on him, she would never know. Nobody ate their own beef in a cattle country. Even the biggest rancher had eaten the next man's beef when he needed to. But it was now a crime to do that if you were a little man. If you were a big man and didn't need the meat, then that was another matter.

She called and called, but hearing no more shots, she returned to the house and shut the door behind her. The child was still crying.

The three men dismounted in the yard and Church led the way onto the stoop and knocked with the butt of his quirt on the door. Mrs. Rigden, pale and distraught as usual, answered the knock.

"Evenin', Mrs. Rigden. Mr. Rigden around?"

"Evening, Mr. Church. He's in the office. You go right along there."

He thanked her and touched his hat and led the way along the stoop to the office door. Here he knocked and received a growled order to enter. He went in and the others followed him.

The smell of whiskey and cigar smoke hit them after the cold damp night air.

Hardy Rigden was slumped in a chair behind the big old roll-top desk. He had been drinking heavily. He was never seen after noon when he hadn't been. He was a man of medium height and middle-aged with wild eyes and untidy short hair. He was heavy in the shoulders and was starting to put on weight around the middle.

A well chewed cigar smoldered between his sensual lips.

"Well?" he drawled.

He had always been a man of power. He knew it and he saw to it that others knew it. He had always had his own way and he dominated his world. His family, of which there were many, for his sense of importance if nothing else demanded that he have a strong retinue, feared and respected him.

"It's done," Church said.

He reached in a drawer and tossed them money which they deftly caught.

"Church, you git back into town. You got your alibi rigged?"

"Yes."

"Strange and you, Willy, you've been in the bunkhouse all evening. Remember that."

"Yes, sir," they said.

"All right," he told them in dismissal.

Even though they knew him, they expected more than that. Church who had never before been in awe of any man, surprised himself by keeping silent and turning to leave the room with the others.

Rigden poured himself another drink as the door closed behind them. He tossed it off and his mind went back to the early years in Texas, remembering how he had started with a running iron. It had been a careless iron and many a maverick had been branded on another man's range. There had been shootings a-plenty, always there had been shooting wherever Rigden had gone. But in those days there had been only him and his hired men. Now he had the men but, better than that, he had his sons. There was nothing like having sons.

Burt, the eldest, was an enigma, but he did as he was told and Hardy Rigden liked that. A big dour man coming up for thirty and not yet married. That was the one thing that worried Rigden about Burt. It wasn't healthy for a bull not to have a cow at that age.

Now Brett, the second, was a different matter. He had the same wild streak as his father. Rigden laughed out loud with delight when he thought of his second son. There was a real Texas heller if there was ever one. He could drink, shoot, ride and whore with the best of them. He had so many different women, he didn't need a wife. How often Margaret, the ladylike Margaret, Rigden's wife, had begged Rigden to let up on the boy. Allow him to learn civilised ways, she begged. They were not in Texas any more. This was the north and men behaved differently up here. This was the cold north.

Sure, it was. Rigden sighed for the hot dusty trails of the brasada, the warm still nights, the endless brush. There was something about south-west Texas that got into a man's blood and stayed there forever. And they had driven him out. So Texas wasn't here in the north, wasn't it? By God, he'd show them. He'd plant Texas and its ways up here among these cold northerners. He had started. Tonight, he had started with that miserable nester. He'd show them that it was death to plant yourself on the edge of

Rigden's empire and to try nibbling it away. You couldn't tell him that every nester wasn't a rustler. He knew cow-thieves. Hadn't he started out as one himself?

Woman's heels sounded on the planks of the stoop outside and the door opened.

Margaret, his wife stood there.

He looked at her with some distaste. He hated anything he couldn't break or mold to his own liking. Sure, she was obedient enough, she never spoke out of turn, but none of that fooled him. He knew that the spirit inside her was untouched. He would never reach that.

She stopped and he saw the look of disapproval on her face because he had been drinking too much.

"Hardy."

"Yes." He poured himself another generous tot of whiskey and enjoyed the look it brought to her face.

"It's Brett."

"What about him?"

"I'm worried about him."

"Why? What's happened?"

"That's the trouble. I don't know. He's been gone five whole days."

"Hell, is that all? The kid's on the town. He's young — let him enjoy himself."

"He's wild. Anything could have happened to him. You know him."

"Sure, I know him. I should, I'm his daddy. You leave Brett to me, woman. He wouldn't thank us for interferin'. Let him enjoy himself."

Quietly, she said: "What sort of a father are you?"

He was silent under the shock of her speaking to him in that way. He hadn't heard that tone in her voice for twenty years. For a moment, he couldn't believe his ears.

"What's that?" he demanded, pushing his chair back.

"I said 'What kind of a father are you?' You encourage the boy. You egg him on in his wildness. You want him to be like you."

He reared to his feet, his face mottled, his eyes enflamed.

"Shut your God-damned mouth," he shouted. "Shut it. What in hell's wrong with wanting him like me? Why shouldn't he be like me?"

"You want him to end up like you? With the whole world turned against him? You want him to end up with blood on his hands like you?"

"You're meddlin' in a man's world now, woman. Keep out of it."

She stood up straight and, white-faced, looked him in the eye.

"Maybe I'm meddling because I don't want any part of your man's world. It was your man's world down in Texas. A world of violence."

"You talkin' crazy. Of course, there's violence. How else can a man hold on to what he has?"

"You're starting it all over. This is going to be like Texas when I thought maybe up here you would alter your ways."

His fury made the vein in his temple

stand out blue against the purple of his face. He spoke through his clenched yellow teeth.

"What's so wrong with my ways? They've got me where I am. They've got me on top of the world. I'm the biggest man in this country."

She shot her words straight back at him, almost as venomously as he had spoken and though he didn't show it, she shook him.

"The most hated man in the country."

He came around the desk toward her and for a moment she thought that he would strike her. She could not prevent herself from cringing away from him.

"There ain't a cattleman in this territory who don't respect me, who don't come to me for advice, who don't come to me when they want something done."

"You're talking of the big men. What of the little men, the ordinary people?"

"I don't have no time for little

people. They're just somethin' that gits under a man's feet. Don't talk to me about little people. They don't count."

She braced herself against the wall. She had stepped back away from him and could go no further.

"One day you'll find they do count. They count more than you think."

Softly, he told her: "You git outa here before I do you a harm."

"All I want is for you to look for the boy in town. Bring him home."

She went to the door and opened it. She was physically afraid of him and showed it, yet he knew that her fear of him was no more than skin deep. He noticed her consciously for the first time in years. She was the woman who had borne all his children and kept his house, but for the first time for years he saw that she hated him. But that wouldn't make any difference. Margaret was loyal deep in her very nature. She was his wife and would never be anything else.

She stepped out onto the stoop and he heard her footsteps receding. He went to the desk and poured himself another drink. He drank avidly and slammed the glass down on the desk top. Maybe he'd made a mistake in Margaret years back. He shouldn't have married a lady, but a big strong farm wench. A big dumb Swede, say, who would have kept his bed warm and given him sons and no sass. What in hell had gotten into Margaret all of a sudden? Silence for years and now this. It was Brett, of course. The boy was the one most like him and she hated that, though she doted on the boy. None of her children had meant what Brett had.

Except maybe Jim.

He had been the son between Brett and Burt in age.

Rigden sagged into the chair, suddenly overcome by the old grief. He hadn't thought about Jim in months now. But here he was back fresh in his mind as if he had died only yesterday.

Rigden hadn't been run out of Texas. He hadn't been run out because he had hanged those three mangy hide-hunters, because he had found the law ineffectual and taken it into his own hands. He had left Texas of his own free-will because he couldn't bear to stay in the land that had seen the end of his favorite son. He had come north for the sole purpose of forgetting the way Jim had died.

The bastards had put a rope around Jim's neck and strangled him to death. He never knew who. How could he tell when he had so many enemies?

He wondered for a moment at the fact that men hated him.

They were all fools. It was jealousy and fear that drove them to hate him. He was smart and he was strong. Other strong men didn't hate him because they didn't fear him. It was only the little men that ever wanted him dead.

And tonight a little man had died. That would show the rest of them.

They would get the message all right. They would know that Hardy Rigden was as tough and mean up here in the north as he had been down in Texas.

2

McALLISTER looked at the land and found it good.

This is what I've wanted all my life and now I've gotten it, he thought. At last he had a place where he could put down roots. The wandering days were over.

He watched his two riders hazing the bunch of unbroken horses into the corral and nodded to himself with satisfaction. After they had been topped off, he would sell them at a good price to the army. Hard cash was what he wanted to see him through the coming winter.

He strolled toward the corral, watching the horses, noting their action and deciding that the little bay had bottom, but the coyote dun was one that he would save for himself. It looked strong enough to carry his weight without tiring.

Pete whooped the last horse through the gate and turned back, grinning with pleasure. Ruiz, the little Mexican rider, was already unsaddling on the outside of the corral. Both were good men who knew their jobs. McAllister considered that he was lucky to have them, even though Ruiz was wanted by some lawman or other and Pete would sometimes disappear for days on end on some mysterious errand.

Ruiz slipped the gate poles into place.

Pete halted his horse and was about to step down from the saddle when he looked south and said: "Rider come." The other two men looked, but they could see nothing. But Pete was all Minneconjou Sioux and McAllister reckoned he could smell a white man a mile off.

Ruiz chuckled.

"This, Pete," he said, "he 'ave eyes like a 'awk, I think."

Pete led the two horses away to

the small starve-out where the saddle stock were kept. McAllister continued to look south, wondering who might be coming to his place. Visitors were rare birds up this way. Pete was back by the time the big man saw the small moving dot. They waited, watching the dot grow into a horseman pushing his mount hard. Pretty soon they knew the man from the horse, a shaggy bay with a white blaze on its forehead and one white stocking. This was Whittaker from Bayard's Creek. He and Tom Holley had small places not far from each other. McAllister had shared a jug or two with them now and then.

The horse that came into the yard was lathered and the man was tired. Whittaker got down stiffly and came toward them. He said their names and shook hands.

McAllister said: "Come on inside an' eat. It's only bach food, but it's all we have to offer."

"Thanks," the man said, "but I ain't

stoppin'. I come to tell you about Tom Holley."

"What happened to him?"

"That's it. We don't know. Nobody ain't seen him for two full days. Not hide nor hair."

They stared at him.

"Why come an' tell me?" McAllister asked.

"Because we can make a pretty good guess what happened."

"What's that?"

"The Association."

McAllister was puzzled. "I don't get you," he said.

"A week back the Association warned him if he didn't clear out they'd settle his hash. He wasn't the only one to get the warning. But they threatened us before an' nothin' happened."

"An' you come out here to me."

Whittaker's face was so distressed that McAllister would not have been surprised to see him burst into tears.

"We reckoned they killed him."

"Killed him?" McAllister raised his

eyebrows. "What makes you think that?"

"Rigden's the Association around here. We all know that. An' we know Rigden's reputation."

McAllister knew that. He had heard of Rigden in Texas right over in Arizona. But the man had been quiet since he had been in the north. There had been a drunken brawl or two, a nester beaten, but nothing more.

"When was Holley seen last?" he asked.

"He ride into town. Jake Parsons at the store seen him. Sheriff saw him ride outa town. He should of reached home after dark. But he didn't. Hell, his wife is nigh outa her mind. There's two kids. Christ, I don't know what to do, McAllister."

"If the sheriff knows, what's he goin' to do about it?"

"He says he can't do nothin'. That's a pretty well-used trail and anyhow it rained since Tom come along it. Trackin's out."

McAllister looked at Pete.

"Could you pick up his sign, Pete?"

The Indian nodded.

"Try."

McAllister made up his mind. He would try to help find Tom Holley and then he would come home. That would be the end of it. He didn't want to get mixed up in any range trouble. He was strictly peaceable now.

"Ruiz," he said, "put that horse in the corral and pick out a fresh one for Whittaker. Will, we'll go inside and get some grub under our belts and ride."

There were clouds overhead, but the rain held off. It wasn't cold enough for coats and there was a hush about the country as though rain would fall at any minute. McAllister sat his horse and watched Pete at work. The Indian was sniffing around at the edge of the trail. McAllister reckoned the chances were it had happened around here someplace. Mrs. Holley had heard a shot. Folks didn't go shooting around here regardless. If there had been no rain, it would have been easy for Pete, but he was having trouble now. He had been peering around at the ground on either side of the trail for nearly an hour without getting anywhere. But he hadn't given up yet.

Suddenly, the Indian stopped and looked toward McAllister. He nodded and McAllister walked his horse toward him.

"Horse here," Pete said. "Two, three, mebbe four. Don't know. Go that way." He pointed east. "Goddam, too much rain." He went back to the trail and stopped over it, searching every inch of a patch about ten feet square with his eyes. After maybe fifteen minutes, he picked something up from the rutted path of the trail and ran with it to McAllister and handed it to him. McAllister saw that it was a used .44 shell. He nodded and put it in his pocket.

"Let's go," he said. "We look either for a dead body or for timber."

"Timber?" Whittaker asked. "Why timber?"

"Rigden's a hangin' man," McAllister told him with a grim face. Whittaker went white. McAllister turned his horse, Pete climbed aboard his and led the way slowly into the east.

They found Tom Holley the following day, hanging stiffly with his head on one side. Will Whittaker got quickly from his horse and started retching. McAllister didn't follow suit but he knew how he felt.

"Pete," he said, "cut him down. I want that rope."

The Indian obeyed him. The corpse made an unpleasant sound as it hit the ground.

McAllister took the rope from around the dead man's neck and carefully coiled it before he hung it from his saddle by the rope strap. They wrapped the corpse in their slickers and tied it so that it would ride neatly on the back of one of their horses. McAllister's being the biggest and strongest they chose that and loaded it. The big sorrel didn't like the smell of death any more than the men did and it acted up a little, but after a while they were headed for town. As they rode they debated whether to take the body home to Mrs. Holley, but McAllister was against that. Whittaker headed for the Holley's place to tell the dead man's wife of the finding, McAllister sent Pete on home, for there was work to be done, and McAllister headed for town and the sheriff.

Over a bottle in town Willy was saying to Strange: "They won't find the body in a month of Sundays. Not after that rain."

Strange looked across the table at him.

"You'll open your mouth once too often, Willy. Just shut it and keep it shut. You don't know nothin' about no dead man."

Willy grinned. With a liberal dose of whiskey the strange feeling he had

had in the pit of his stomach since the killing had gone away. He felt pretty good now, but he couldn't help picturing over and over the look on Holley's face as the rope tightened around his neck. He poured them each another drink. He had plenty of money and was going to get good and properly drunk. Like that sonovabitch's boss's son yonder with his head down on the table, lost in drunken sleep.

The sheriff, it was said, was a nester's man.

McAllister knew him by sight but had never spoken to him before. The lawman's name was Zane Bright. He had the lugubrious face of a bloodhound. His eyes, his cheeks and his mustache drooped. He was not one of your hard riding, gun-toting Western sheriffs. He was a political man. He ran his office pretty well for one in a raw territory. He didn't like cattlemen overly and he had been put into office by the votes of the townspeople and the settlers. He knew his limitations. He tried to uphold the law in a country that was dominated by the money and power of the big cattle companies and it was not an easy task. He walked a tightrope and he knew it.

He was the owner of the Bright Emporium, the biggest store in the territory and he was a man of means. In spite of his high office, he was still to be found most mornings waiting on customers in his store. He was a trader by nature and he hated to be long away from trading. He was waiting on a lady when McAllister walked into the store and said: "Mr. Bright?"

"Yes."

"I have a dead man outside."

The sheriff didn't bat an eyelid. He looked at McAllister dully and remarked: "Izzat so?"

"Where do you want I should put him?"

"How'd he die?"

"Somebody hung him from a tree."

The sheriff turned to his pale

lady customer and said: "Excuse me, ma'am." He called to a young man: "Harry, come and wait on Mrs. Jamieson, will you?"

The sheriff took off his white apron and put on his coat and hat. He walked out onto the street with McAllister and sadly viewed the closely wrapped body on the back of the sorrel horse.

"Who is he?"

"Tom Holley."

Bright took a match from his pocket and chewed on it a little.

"Threats made against him, if'n I remember right. Still that don't make no clear cut case, the way I see it. Walk down to the undertaker's with me, will you?"

They walked the horse down the street to the undertaker's with people watching them curiously. When they were in the undertaker's and the dead man was laid out on a bench, the sheriff nodded his head and said: "That's Tom Holley, all right. Come back to my office. We'd best chew the fat a mite about this, if you ain't hurryin' off."

They walked back to the store, went through the store into Bright's tiny office at the rear. The sheriff poured them each a drink, offered McAllister a cigar which was refused and lit one himself.

"I know who done this," he said. "You know it. Every homesteader in the section knows it. But we can't prove nothin'. But we have to make a try, I reckon. I'd best send somebody up there to ask questions. You willin' to be a deputy?"

"Sorry," McAllister told him.

"Pity. I heard about you. Howsomever, I'll find somebody."

They talked a little longer before McAllister left and walked along to the Cattleman for a drink. Since he had been into town nearly a year back the whole country had filled up and the conditions were reflected in the saloon. When he had been here before the place had been a large empty room with a plank on a barrel for the bar.

Now there were chairs and tables, a fine oak bar and two busy men behind it. Over their shoulders he could see rows of fancy bottles backed by a large mirror. The owner had made money and raised his standards.

The place was full of men, some leaning on the bar, others trying their luck at cards and other games at the tables. The air was blue with smoke and loud with the sound of voices.

McAllister thought: *I'll have just one drink, then I'll get a feed for my horse.* He elbowed his way to the bar, bellied up to it and called for a whiskey and a beer. They came. He knocked the whiskey back in one before he made slow work of the beer. The drink tasted good after the long miles. He leaned his back on the bar and looked around.

Near him was a table with three men sitting at it. One, doing the talking, was a young man with a foxy face that needed a shave. The other was older, square-set and with a graven face, saying little. McAllister knew him. His memory for faces never failed him. The name was Strange and he had run him in over some gun-trouble down in Crewsville, Arizona, five years back. A small time gun-hand. The third man at the table had just taken his head from the table-top where he looked to have been sleeping off a long and prolonged drunk. The face was young, but the look on it was as old as time. It looked utterly debauched.

Young fool, McAllister thought.

He turned his head and saw another face he knew. This man was playing cards at a table. This was a man he knew better, a man he respected. His name was Church. He was now a stock-grower's detective. Not so long ago he had been a chief scout for the army down in Arizona. He and McAllister had gone on a long scout together toward the end of the Geronimo trouble. They had seen hard times and such times revealed men to each other. McAllister reckoned that he knew Joe Church as well as any other man on earth.

He turned and downed his beer and when he turned from the bar again, he saw that Church had laid down his cards and risen to his feet.

He stepped across the room and said: "Hiya, Joe."

Church turned quickly, tensed.

Then he relaxed at the sight of McAllister. The smile touched his mouth and after that came into his eyes. The smile became a grin and he held out a hand to McAllister.

"Rem," he said. "Real nice to see you."

They shook, both of them remembering back, remembering how they had ridden, fought and been scared together.

McAllister said: "Could you use a drink?"

"Sure could."

They stepped up to the bar and McAllister called for drinks. They drank and Church said: "You're a long way from home, Rem."

McAllister smiled.

"Right on my doorstep, Joe. I'm raisin' horses here."

Church raised his eyebrows in surprise.

"You mean you settled down? Don't tell me. You'll be tellin' me you gotten yourself married next."

"I ain't gone the whole hog, yet. But I'm havin' a whole heap of fun with the hosses."

"Where at?"

"Over in the Creek country. You must come over."

He watched a shadow pass over the other's face.

"I'd like that." There was no enthusiasm in the man's voice. "I'm with the Cattlemen's Association now."

"I heard that."

They were both being cautious now.

The door slammed open and there was an eddy of movement around it. McAllister turned his head and saw that several men had entered and were looking around the place. His whole attention was however taken by one man. He was of average height and dressed in the rough clothes of a working cowman, blue flannel shirt with a cowskin vest, faded blue levis tucked into knee-high boots. A gun hung from the belt at his waist in an old and worn holster. It was the man's reckless, swaggering air that caught McAllister's attention, the wild look in his eyes. It was the look of a man who was barely under control. Here was violence.

From beside McAllister, Church: "Hardy Rigden."

Rigden caught sight of the drunken young man at the table and headed straight for him. The boy turned and saw him and started in what looked like fright.

Halting, Rigden tucked his thumbs into his pants' top and said: "You had long enough in town, boy. Fork your hoss and git."

The boy said: "I ain't through yet, pa."

The man caught him by the scruff of his neck and hauled him to his feet.

"Don't give me no sass," he said. "Git." And with that he propelled him toward the door.

Several men laughed.

Rigden swung on them in fury.

"Nobody don't laugh," he said.

The laughs died.

Rigden glared around the place. For a moment, his eyes met Church's and, for a moment, they rested on McAllister. Then he turned and walked out. The other men followed him and the silence that had fallen was broken and the hubbub of talk went on.

"A real rooster," McAllister said.

Church laughed dryly and remarked: "You can say that again."

"They reckon he's the Association in this neck of the woods."

"He sure means to clean the country up," Church said, "if that's what you mean. He's goin' to stop rustlin'."

"It sure looks like it."

Church gave him a quick look.

"How come?"

"I found a dead man out on the range."

"What kind of a dead man?"

A hung man." McAllister didn't miss the deadly stillness that had come over his friend. "He'd been strung up. Been there a couple of days. He'd been shot too to make sure of him."

"Rustler?"

"How should I know? All I know is, he was a kind of neighbour of mine. Tom Holley. Quiet, peaceable feller. Minded his own business."

"Did he eat his own beef?"

"Who does in cow country?"

Church leaned forward earnestly.

"Times're changed, Rem. You eat another man's beef these days an' that's rustlin'. Things've got so bad, we got to stop this cow-stealin' dead."

"Dead's the word," McAllister said. "I don't know nothin' about this

Holley or whatever his name is," Church said.

"I didn't say you did, Joe."

"I'm a range detective. I find the culprits then I start a due process of the law."

"The only trouble is," McAllister said, "that the law around here is nester's law."

"Are you suggestin' anything, Rem?"

"I'm suggestin' nothin'. It ain't my quarrel. I'm strictly on the sidelines. I raise hosses. Cattle ain't my concern. Have another drink?"

They drank again. The foxy-faced young man and Strange got up from their table and left. Church and McAllister small-talked for ten minutes and then McAllister left. He took his horse along to the livery stable and saw that it had a good feed. Then he headed along Main to the store to buy some ammunition for his Henry repeater.

3

SHE caught McAllister's eye at once, just as she had caught the eye of every man on the street.

She wasn't a girl any more. But then young girls either didn't interest McAllister at his age or they were out of his reach. He was never sure which. But this woman stopped him dead in his tracks and he told himself: *That's the woman for me*.

He was astonished at the interior decision. He who had fought shy of any permanent liaison with a woman since his wife had died. Nobody had ever been able to take her place and he thought never would. But now, after one look at this woman, he made himself a statement like that.

Having made such a decision, he had to do something about it. Life was short and it was his axiom to act now. Tomorrow might be too late. Such an axiom had got him into a lot of trouble in his time, but it had gotten him a whole lot of fun too.

He gave the woman a good second look.

She was, he decided, in her late twenties. The front of her red-gold hair was bleached by the sun. Her dress and her bonnet were blue and that brought out the startling blue of her eyes. Her skin, though faintly tanned, had not been ruined by the climate. Yet she belonged to the open air, that much a glance could tell him. She would, he thought, look wonderful on the back of a horse.

Her figure was full and good. Her hips were firm and wide, yet her waist was as slender as a man could desire. She sat very upright on the buggy seat and pretended that she didn't know what she must have known — that every man in sight was looking at her.

He stepped down from the sidewalk and lifted his hat politely.

"Excuse me, ma'am," he said. She looked down at him and the look she gave him made his heart miss a beat. Just like a brash kid, he thought.

"Yes?" she said and a golden eyebrow raised itself ever so slightly.

"May I ask if you're Miss Henrietta Mayo of Virginia City?"

"No, sir, I am not."

"Forgive me my mistake."

"Of course." She raised her eyes and stared straight ahead. For her the interview was at an end. McAllister knew that it had barely started.

"It's quite a natural mistake," he said, "when you think of all the circumstances."

The eyes came back to him again. She had flushed slightly and was starting to look a little annoyed.

Foolishly, she said: "And what are the circumstances?" McAllister chuckled to himself. This was his lead. The woman was lost.

"There was this friend of mine. He knew this Miss Henrietta Mayo of

Virginia City. He told me that she had hair like spun gold and eyes of the clearest cornflower blue. He told me too that she was the most beautiful lady he had ever seen. So naturally, when I saw you a-sittin' there, I thought of what my friend had told me and I thought: This must be her. She. Well, you see what I mean, ma'am. A perfectly natural mistake."

Her lower lip trembled. Whether with amusement or anger, he didn't know.

"Thank you for the compliment, sir," she said in an extraordinarily firm voice, "and now I would be obliged if you would walk on."

"Impossible," said McAllister.

"May I ask why?"

McAllister became aware that she was watching the street.

"If I walked on, I might never see you again," he said. "And that is something I don't aim to happen, ma'am. My old daddy always used to say, life is short, if you see something you want, son, why, you up and take it or somebody else will."

She was looking over his shoulder at something behind him and she was frightened. The realization came to him with something like a shock. She was not frightened of him, but for him.

"For pity's sake," she said, her voice suddenly changing, "walk on."

"Is something bothering you, ma'am?" he asked, wanting to look behind him.

"Yes, sir. You are."

He heard the sound of bootheels and the jingle of spurs behind him. There were several men there. The sudden terror was in the woman's eyes.

A hand caught hold of McAllister's arm and spun him around. The grip stayed on it and he looked down into the eyes of Hardy Rigden.

My God, he thought, *have I been talking to this man's wife?*

Rigden said: "Move on, bub." The tone he used was one reserved for saddle tramps in that country. The look went with it.

McAllister glanced beyond the man and saw the others. They were a tough and mean bunch.

He said: "Little man, take your hand off'n my arm or I'll knock your teeth down your throat."

The little man bit was unnecessary because Rigden stood all of six feet. He just happened to be shorter than McAllister. The threat was uncalled for, but the sight of the man and his arrogance was too much for the big man. This was a man who ruled his world and McAllister had spent a lifetime seeing that such men did not rule *his*. Besides, he didn't like being taken down a peg in front of any woman, least of all this one.

Rigden fell back a pace in complete astonishment.

"What?" he said. "Do you know who I am?"

McAllister brushed the hand from his arm and said: "Yes. You're Hardy Rigden. You was run out of Texas."

He saw the rage come into the man's

eyes. He didn't have to be clairvoyant to know that was fighting talk in Rigden's language. The man signalled the blow that came all the way from Cheyenne. It was such that it could have felled an ox. Rigden was used to knocking men down. He had done it for years and he had never failed.

McAllister stepped aside from it. His own hand came out as fast as a spitting cobra and the insult of it was that his hand was open. The slap could have been heard clear across Main. Rigden's head was batted on one side, he staggered and his ears sang. The horse in the buggy reared high and the woman screamed.

Rigden took two paces backward, his face livid and contorted.

"Take him," he screamed.

The man nearest McAllister reached instinctively for his gun, but McAllister was moving in on him before he made the move. The gun-wrist was gripped and poor Willy was heaved helplessly from his feet. He yelled and the gun clattered onto the sidewalk. It went off with a roar and Willy took off with a howl. McAllister whirled him around wildly once and threw him with all his strength. Hardy Rigden and a man running in on McAllister were hurled from their feet. They went down into the dust as McAllister charged with calculated fury into the other pair. As his old daddy said: When you don't know what to do — charge.

One of these men took a swipe at the big man and sank his fist into his belly. McAllister gasped and smashed his fist into the fellow's face. As he went down the other man leapt onto McAllister's back. McAllister bent down violently and threw him clear. He landed on his back on the edge of the sidewalk and screamed agonizingly that his back was broken.

Willy and Rigden got to their feet.

Willy dove for his fallen gun, for he thought in terms of guns and Rigden charged blindly, roaring his rage like a goaded bull.

With a surge of fierce joy, McAllister went to meet him, side-stepping at the last minute and tripping the man onto his face, but not before he had clipped him smartly behind the ear.

As Willy landed on his belly and got his hand on his gun, McAllister took two long strides and stamped down on his hand with a cowman's bootheel. Willy gave a prolonged moan and fainted. McAllister scooped up the gun which was handy because he didn't wear one of his own these days, only carrying the Henry in his saddleboot.

Rigden came to his feet. His face was flecked with dust and blood. The other man whom McAllister had thrown over his shoulder got to his feet and swept his gun from leather. McAllister cocked and fired. You didn't fool around with a man with a gun in his hand.

The heavy ball from the Colt .45 caught him high in the shoulder, swung him around and dumped him down into the dust.

Rigden, about to heave gun from

leather, let it stay.

McAllister said: "Take it out awful easy, mister, or I'm liable to kill you."

For a moment, McAllister thought the man would have a fit then and there. He stood speechless, choking on his inhuman rage. Then slowly he took hold of the gun butt with forefinger and thumb and dropped it on the ground.

"Put that gun away," he said finally, "and finish this like a man."

"You've got guts," McAllister told him, "I'll give you that."

"Finish it," the man begged.

McAllister laughed and the laugh goaded the man.

"You're old enough to have more sense. I'd kill you."

"Put down the gun and see. There ain't a man alive I can't whup."

Bootheels sounded on the sidewalk. The sheriff appeared, apron flapping and gun in hand.

At the sight of McAllister he said: "Oh, it's you."

Rigden pointed a finger that shook with rage.

"Arrest that man, sheriff. He assaulted me."

McAllister grinned.

"Sure," he said. "I assaulted all five of 'em."

Bright glanced from McAllister to Rigden, then regarded the fallen men somewhat quizzically. He looked rather afraid that the gun in his hand might go off. He turned to the bystanders.

"Anybody see this?" he demanded.

They shook their heads; one man said he had only just come up. Bright said: "As I expected. Well, Rigden, I suggest you pick up that wounded man and get him down to the doctor's."

Rigden shouted: "You mean this man is goin' to get away with a deliberate shooting."

Bright asked; "What you got to say to that, McAllister?"

McAllister grinned angelically.

"Only that I had to borrow a gun from one of 'em to shoot it," he said.

The sheriff made an impatient sound.

"I might have known it," he said. "Come on, Rigden, get off the street. I've got work to get back to."

"Goddam storekeeper," Rigden growled. "You ain't heard the last of this. They hear me talk in the capital. There's goin' to be plenty said about this."

He picked up his fallen gun and thrust it away into leather. Then he climbed onto the buggy seat and picked up the lines. He yelled to the horse and sent it careering down the street. The woman was thrown against the back of the seat and had to cling to the rail to stay aboard. McAllister lifted his hat as she passed and she cast him one wild glance as she went. Even then she managed to look beautiful.

The wounded man was sitting up and saying in quite a cheerful voice that he thought he was dying. Willy stirred and sat up, white-faced.

McAllister handed him his gun and said: "Put it away, little boy."

He and Bright walked down the street together.

"Who," McAllister asked, impatient for the answer, "was the lady?"

Bright gave him a knowing look.

"Rose Carmichael," he said.

"What relation to Rigden?"

"Sister-in-law. His wife's sister."

McAllister gave a sigh of relief. There was still a chance.

4

ON the way home, McAllister called in at Whittaker's place. To get there, he had to pass the Holley sod-house. The place was deserted.

The first thing he asked Whittaker was: "Mrs. Holley pull out?"

"Yeah. Went to her brother's in Cheyenne. Didn't have a chance stayin' on here. Who's next, McAllister?"

"Search me. But there'll be more, you can be sure of that."

Whittaker invited him in for a meal, but he said his thanks and pushed on. He wanted to be home. He always wanted to be home now. That was probably the effect of old age, he thought. That and being struck that way by a woman. But he thought about her, just the same. He saw her face in front of him as he rode, seeing her sitting beside that animal of a man Rigden.

When he reached the house, he found Pete and Ruiz busy breaking the horses in. The coyote dun, they had left for him as he requested. He started to work right away, doing what he always did with a new horse, letting it get to know him. The dun was pretty wild and had never known a saddle. His mother had been a cute little mare with roughly the same marking and she had been a stayer. He hoped that she would give him more like this. He nearly got kicked to death for his pains, working on the dun, but he snubbed the animal down close and worked on it unhurriedly, gently and firmly. It took him four days before he could get astride without being bucked off and five before he could ride it without trouble with nothing more than a hackamore on it. And all the time he dreamed of upgrading his stock and breeding real class and he dreamed of having the woman there in the house with him.

Then on the sixth day, while he was working with the dun, Church rode in.

The first thing that McAllister noticed was the horse he was on, which was natural. It was a beautiful and flawless sorrel with more than a little Arab blood in it as shown by its delicate profile and its neat round barrel. It had pace and endless bottom. It was small, but it didn't lose anything by that.

McAllister climbed through the corral fence and walked toward the man.

"Rem."

"Joe."

McAllister couldn't take his eyes from the horse.

"Man," he said, "if that hoss was a stud, I'd buy him."

Church smiled.

"But I wouldn't sell."

"'Light," McAllister told him and the Association man swung down. They didn't talk then. When the sorrel had been unsaddled and turned into the starve-out, fed and watered, the two men sat on the stoop and took a drink.

"What brings you out this way?" McAllister asked.

"Association business."

"So you stopped off for a chin-wag."

"My business is here, Rem."

Church looked grave. If McAllister didn't know the man better, he would have said that he was uneasy.

"Here?"

"Yeah. I hate to do this."

"You hate to do what?"

McAllister sat forward in his chair. He had never seen Church look uncomfortable before. There was no change in the expression on his face, but there was embarrassment in every line of his body. He looked McAllister in the eye and then stared at the distant horizon, the blue rim of the mountains.

"You an' me rode a fair number of

trails together, Rem. You know me. I never believed in much an' if I did believe in anythin', I wasn't one that knew how to talk about it."

McAllister said: "But you found somethin' to believe in now."

"Yes, I did. There's a war on."

McAllister was all attention.

"I didn't notice it," he said.

"There's always war where there's cows and cowmen. There was war when Texas wanted to take the longhorns through Kansas. There was war on the Staked Plains with the Indians when we first run cows in there. Then there was war with the sheepmen. Now there's war with the rustlers. There's a war against fences. We're fightin' for the world of cattle, we're fightin' for the old days, Rem."

McAllister frowned. He looked hard at his friend, puzzled.

"Strikes me," he said, "you have to go mighty careful here. You start lookin' so hard from one angle, you forget there's another."

"You mean I'm takin' sides."

"That's what I mean."

"Can you tell me of a time when a man didn't have to take sides. There's a right an' a wrong."

"You sure you ain't on the wrong side?"

The look that Church gave him contained something like horror. The man was plainly and honestly shocked.

"You said I was takin' sides. Sure I am. I'm taking sides for the right against the wrong. The old ways're the best, Rem. They're the ways I growed up in. Hell, the land's swarmin' with late-comers, with men that don't give a damn for the country. You can't ride a day without seein' the smoke of their chimneys. Dirt farmers, shirttail cattlemen, sod-busters, sheepmen. They're all crowdin' in to finish off the cattlemen."

"You're wrong, Joe." McAllister's voice was firm. "They're maybe finishin' off the big cattlemen. An' who are these big fellers? They're companies financed from Europe and the east. They ain't the west, they ain't this country. These little fellers you don't think so much of, they'll become the west. They put down roots — "

Church interrupted him angrily.

"Not while I can sit a hoss or tote a gun, man."

McAllister leaned back in his chair. It came to him that nobody could ever get through to Joe Church any more. He was a man committed.

"So you hired your gun out to the Association. You're goin' to gun down anybody that stands in the way of the foreign capital."

"I reckon I don't care for the way you say that," Church said and the words were spoken through his teeth. "I'm remembering we was friends, Rem. I'm tryin' hard. I come to warn you."

"Warn me of what?"

"The Association's seeing the nesters off. They'll get around to hombres your size. Can't you see what I'm tellin' you, boy?"

"You're sayin' my name's on the list."

"That's what I'm sayin'."

McAllister made a sound of disgust.

"My God," he said, "what's happened to you, Joe?" Light entered his brain. He thought of Tom Holley, he saw again the sight of the man hanging from the tree and heard the sound of his body hitting the hard ground when he was cut down. "Holley," he said.

Church's eyes would not meet his.

McAllister leaned forward and spoke vehemently.

"You killed him, Joe. You hung him."

Church made a gesture with a hand loosely.

"He was a cow-thief. They've always hung. He was trash."

McAllister said: "I drank with that trash. I bought my beef from him. I played with his kids. He had a wife and two kids. Don't that mean nothin' to you?"

"Don't give me that stuff," Church

came back with as much vehemence. "There has to be law and order. The sheriff's on the side of the rustlers. He's a nester sheriff. If he won't enforce the law, then we will."

"You mean you're above the law."

"I mean the time for sentiment is past. This is war and there're bound to be casualties."

McAllister stood up and looked down on his friend.

"There ain't no use talkin' to you, Joe. You're too far gone."

Church stood and measured nearly as tall as McAllister.

"I come here with a good intention, Rem," he said soberly. "I thought maybe you'd remember the old days. I come with an offer."

"An offer?"

"I'd hoped you'd join us."

"Hire my gun?"

"You make it sound like it was somethin' dirty. This is a crusade, Rem. This'll make history. We're goin' to sweep this country clean. It'll be the old days back again. You don't realize what you're up against."

It began to dawn on McAllister that there was more behind Joe Church's talk than he had at first supposed.

"Come right out with it," he said. "What's goin' to happen?"

Church hesitated. He looked like a man who had said too much in the heat of the moment.

"I can't tell you. I said too much already. But I can repeat what I said. "You don't stand a chance, Rem. If you won't join us, pull out. For old time's sake, don't put your gun on the other side to me."

McAllister drew a long breath and he thought. In a half minute of thought, he saw himself through the problem that he faced, or as much of it as he could see. When he finally spoke, it was softly.

"Joe," he said, "there's only one thing for you to do."

"What's that?"

"You fork your hoss an' you ride.

Next time I see you, I'll know you're on the other side."

They stared at each other, both saddened, the anger gone now.

"That's your final answer?"

"Yeah."

"I did all I could, Rem."

"I reckon you did, Joe."

Church shrugged his shoulders and stepped down from the stoop into the dust of the yard.

5

JOE CHURCH did not return to town after he left the McAllister place. He rode on north, then he swung slowly around to the east and kept on going until night fell. That brought him to a fire by the side of the railroad tracks. There was a fire burning and around it were some half-dozen men. They stirred when Church approached and stepped down from the saddle.

Church walked in among them, checking their faces to make sure they were all there. They all were — Willy, Clegg, Madge, Gafferty and Plenn: all men selected from different ranches. A thrill went through him. This was the beginning of the end. Now he must be sure that every part of the plan fell into place. He greeted them and they fell back to their haunches, talking idly, chewing on the meat they were roasting on sticks over the fire, all pretending that the excitement of the affair did not touch them. He noted that they all wore revolvers at their waists and glancing towards the tied horses on the fringe of the firelight, he saw that each saddleboot carried a repeating rifle. This was part of his army and he was a general.

He took his share of the meat and accepted a cup of hot bitter coffee, not talking. He wanted to think. He pushed the man McAllister from his mind, writing him off as he had written off so many other things from his past.

They waited there an hour, until a man lifted his head and said: "There she is."

They all jerked up their heads and listened.

"You got whistles in your haid, Gafferty," Clegg said.

"I heard her, I tell you."

They all strained their ears. Plenn straightened himself to his feet and said: "It's her all right."

The distant mournful note of the engine's whistle sounded through the night. They were all on their feet.

Church said: "Get them hosses further back, boys. We don't want 'em all tangled up."

The men hurried to obey him, gathering up the lines and leading the horses to the top of a nearby ridge and tying them in the timber there. Next, Church had them rig a rope corral up near the line and by the time they had finished that they could hear the puffing approach of the train and see the brightness of its fire.

The driver had apparently seen their fire. He gave them a couple of short toots on his whistle and started to slow down. The engine was going at no more than a walking pace by the time it came opposite the fire, then, with a great hiss of steam, it halted.

At once a dark figure detached itself

from a long truck and peered about him.

"Church here?" he called.

"Here."

The newcomer was tall and lean and dressed in range clothes.

"Donovan," the man told him and they shook. "The driver don't reckon on hangin' around here. He's jumpy an' I can't say I blame him."

"Got the hosses?" Church demanded.

"Sure. In the first two trucks."

"There's a rope corral yonder. Back up a mite an' we can get 'em straight in. I don't aim to lose any in the dark."

Donovan ran to the engine and shouted to the driver. With loud hisses and groans the engine backed up till many voices told him to 'hold it'.

Two more men appeared from the dark line of trucks. They carried rifles. Church bawled his orders and the side of the first truck was let down. There was silence for a moment and then a horse appeared from the darkness of the vehicle and started on unsteady legs down the ramp. Men went around the other side of the truck and started hammering and yelling. More horses appeared. Church counted twenty of them. By the light of the fire he thought they looked good stock. He felt pleased.

Donovan shouted for the engine to pull up a little and soon another ramp was down and again a small tide of horses flowed from the wagon and the little rope corral was tight with horses and men were spread around the outside to hold them there. The three men off the train fetched their bridles and saddles and then the sides of the wagons were raised, Donovan roared to the engine driver and the train drew slowly away. Within moments there was no other sound but the fading puffing of the engine and the soft night noises of the high prairie, the whicker and movement of horses.

Donovan joined Church in emptying the coffee pot at the fire. They hunkered down and inspected each other.

Church saw a man taller than himself, a man with a face of granite that was lightened only by the gleam of the pale grey eyes. This was a tough one, all right.

"Good hosses," Church said.

"The best that money can buy. What's next?"

"Rigden's place."

"The men?"

"They'll be picked up in town tomorrow. We couldn't manage the passenger train like we did this one. They'll be noticed, but that can't be helped."

"By what I hear, there ain't much opposition."

"Not so far. A nester got himself hung. One or two have moved out. When they see this army the rest'll clear the country."

Donovan laughed and the sound was like steel grating on cold stone.

"An' I kind of looked forward to a

fight. I heard tell this Rigden's a real heller."

Church said: "Some say kill-crazy. But he has the right ideas and he has plenty of spunk. The old breed."

He poured the grounds of the coffee over the fire and scattered the embers, kicking dirt over them. He called to the men and they went for their horses. Donovan and his two men took their ropes into the corral and caught up a horse each. The corral was dismantled and the mounted men kept the loose horses close herded.

Church told the men: "The man that loses a horse, loses a week's pay."

They edged the horses up the ridge with care, knowing that they were spooky after their confinement on the train, keeping them close and watching them like hawks. As soon as he could, Church hit a good pace, knowing that he had to have them safely out of sight before daylight. Nobody in the country must know of their presence here until the time was ripe.

The following day, two things happened that were momentous in the life of Remington McAllister.

The first was the girl.

The sun had been up for some three hours and McAllister was giving a sturdy bay the first taste of the bit. The animal didn't take kindly to the steel in its mouth and the big man had his work cut out. It was Pete as usual who spotted the oncoming rider and with that first cry of warning, McAllister wondered if Joe Church's threat was going to materialize. But Pete's sharp eyes had seen long before McAllister that the rider was a woman.

That had McAllister beaten. What woman would come calling on him. There was something of a flurry among the three men when they saw that the rider wore pants like a man. It was only when she rounded the end of the corral that McAllister realized, in a moment of utter disbelief, that it was Rose Carmichael.

She rode superbly, he saw, with

all the supple grace and ease of the best male rider. Her horse, he noted, was a sorrel fittingly small, neat and beautiful. She wore a flat Mexican hat, a white silk blouse and a short cut-away Mexican vest that was decorated with gold braid. Her pants were well-cut fawn-colored cords and her boots a small version of his own. Her heels lacked spurs.

He got down from the bay, walked to the corral fence and simply stared.

She rode to the other side of the fence, looked down at him without the glimmer of a smile and said: "Good morning, Mr. McAllister."

Ruiz swept his sombrero from his greasy head.

Pete gawked like the savage he was.

McAllister slowly reached his hand to his hat and removed it.

"'Mornin', ma'am."

"Am I welcome to get down?"

He saw that she was strained, on the edge of fear and his wonderment mounted.

"Sure," he said. "'Light. Come onto the stoop out of this sun. Pete, some cold water from the well." He stooped and came through the fence. "Or would you prefer coffee, ma'am?"

She stepped down from her horse and Ruiz took her line from her and tied it to the fence.

"Water will do fine," she said. She headed for the stoop and McAllister followed her. The bravado he had exhibited on the street that morning was notably lacking. She walked ahead of him with head up and her back straight. She was, he guessed, a woman fighting hard to keep control.

He sat her in his rocker and squatted in front of her. Pete came with the water and she thanked him. The Indian returned to join Ruiz at the corral and to stand and stare at the pair on the stoop.

"I expect," she said, in a voice that was too loud and too clear, "you're wondering why I've come."

"I'm wonderin' all right," he said. "But it's no never mind why you came. It's good enough you're here."

There was no mistaking his tone, but she chose to show that she did not understand it.

She looked at him squarely.

"You stood up to Hardy Rigden. I never saw anybody do that before." There wasn't anything he could say to that, so he held his tongue and waited. She seemed to be thinking of her next words. "Were you unaware who he was, Mr. McAllister?"

"Everybody's heard of Hardy Rigden," he said.

"Yet you weren't afraid."

"You're only afraid when you know you can take a beatin'," he said with what he fondly believed was modesty. "I knew those boys couldn't take me, so I wasn't afraid."

"It was as simple as that."

"I reckon."

He thought he saw the suspicion of a smile at the corners of her mouth.

He sat and gazed at her, enraptured. He wondered how he could delay her and keep her here.

"I'll come to the point. Possibly I've been missed at the ranch already."

"You mean you — ?"

"I mean that if Hardy heard I was here, well . . . there would be a certain amount of unpleasantness. I must not stay long. So I'll come to the point straightaway. You're in danger, Mr. McAllister."

"In what way?"

"I can't tell you all the details because I don't know them. If I knew them, it might not be right for me to tell you of them. I owe my brother-in-law a certain amount of loyalty. I suppose." There was some doubt in her voice. "But you're in danger. I heard the men talking when they didn't know I was there. What happened to Tom Holley?"

"Tom Holley?"

"Yes. They said you would get the same treatment that he had."

"You mean you don't know what happened to Holley?"

"No, I don't. But the way the men spoke, it sounded as though it were something unpleasant."

"Very unpleasant. He was hung."

The girl went white and put the back of her hand to her mouth. McAllister wished he hadn't told her.

"But," she whispered, "Hardy would never . . ."

He reached forward and patted her hand.

"But you came to tell me. Why?"

"I couldn't let trouble come to any fellow human, could I?" She looked away toward the hills. "I didn't know what was planned, but I felt that it was something terrible. There's something going on I don't know about. Riders coming in the night, riders going. The men're excited. There's no work being done on the ranch and the Association man, Mr. Church, has been to see Hardy several times. I don't know much about these things, but I feel that Hardy means to make war on the settlers. Is such a thing possible?"

McAllister nodded somberly.

"It's possible," he said. "But why me?"

First there was Joe Church and now, the following day, this girl.

"You ask that?" she said. "Hardy never forgets a grudge. You did to him on the street that day what no man has ever dared. You beat him and made him look a fool."

"It adds," he said, "by what I've heard of the man." He stood up and stretched himself. Looking down at her, he asked: "What sort of life do you lead in that house, Miss Carmichael?"

The very directness of the question startled her.

"That's a very personal question," she replied, coloring slightly.

"It was meant to be. Like you say, time's short. There're things about you I want to know and I want to know 'em now. How do you feel about this brother-in-law of yours?"

She raised her eyes to his and said: "I hate him." It was said quietly and with conviction.

"Do you have to stay there?"

For a moment it seemed that she would not answer the question, but she replied: "I have to. There's my sister. Rigden goes his way and he takes her sons along the same road. I have no choice but to stay."

"A woman like you should be married and have sons of her own."

The flush deepened.

"This conversation is becoming too personal, Mr. McAllister." There was a plea in her voice which he ignored.

"It's goin' to become a sight more personal," he said.

She looked startled again.

"In what way, may I ask?"

"Would you marry a man like me?"

That knocked her all of a heap. She stared at him, eyes wide, she looked away from him and brought her gaze back to bear on him again. She laughed unsteadily.

"Mr. McAllister . . . you're altogether too sudden. I know that Western men . . . Let's forget you ever asked the question."

"No, ma'am, that's something I won't do."

She stood up.

"Mr. McAllister, I came to warn you, nothing more. If I had known . . . why, I would never have come."

He grinned.

"All right," he said, "you'd rather see me hung than have the question asked."

"I don't mean that. I mean . . . oh, I don't know what I mean. You have me confused. You're not fair. Take your warning and I'll go. But you do believe me? You do believe that there is danger for you?"

"I believe it. In fact I'm goin' to act on it."

"I'm glad."

"Now," he said. "Let me see you smile before you go. You've looked like you're at a funeral all the time you've been here. I'd like to remember you smilin'."

And she smiled. Suddenly, she relaxed and showed her teeth and he realized with rush of hope that he was not distasteful to her.

"I must go now," she said, in a low voice, "if I were seen in your part of the country I would be in serious trouble."

"I'll ride you back to your range," he said.

"There's no need."

"It's the least I can do after you comin' all this way for me."

That made it sound personal and she looked away from him. He liked the way she looked when she did that. They walked together to the corral and he roped his chunky bay there, threw a saddle on it and was ready to ride. He would have helped her into the saddle there and then, but a thought came to him and he fetched his Henry rifle from the house in its saddle boot and put it aboard the horse.

He then helped her into the saddle and the touch of her made him realize that she was even more woman than he had at first supposed. Ruiz and Pete stood there rooted in admiration. He and the woman rode off south. They rode across the rich meadow land of the bench with the lush grass swishing at their horses knees and there was not a word spoken between them. Here in the high land, the air was crisp and exhilarating; they breathed it together and for a moment the whole world seemed to be at peace. They reached the creek and followed it along to the steep edge of the bench where it cascaded its way down the rocks and made its way south-east toward the Rigden range. They halted here and watched the waterfall. And here the idea came to McAllister.

"Maybe," he said, "Rigden doesn't want to hang me because I'm a rustler or because I gave him a run for his money in town. Maybe it's the water."

"I don't understand," she told him.

"This creek is Rigden's main source of water," he informed her. "Aw, he has other sources, but if he didn't have this creek the whole of his northern range would be dry. Could be he's scared I'll cut it off."

"Could that be done?" she asked.

He smiled.

"I never thought about it. I'll have to."

She smiled at him in return.

"I have a suspicion that you're a terrible man," she said.

He laughed with the light heart of a boy. He saw a new side to her. This woman could flirt. The look she gave him then sent his heart pounding.

"We're likely," he said, "to be on opposite sides. Would that make any difference to you?"

"In what way?" She frowned in puzzlement, but he knew that she knew what he was talking about.

"Miss Carmichael, you might as well know it now, I'm courtin' you."

Without heat and perhaps with a little bitterness, she said: "And you might as well know, Mr. McAllister, that nobody courts a Rigden lady without Hardy's permission."

"Is that so?" he said, all innocence. "Does that mean you won't see me any more?"

She lowered her eyes.

"It means that I'm old enough and perverse enough to choose my own friends."

Her hand lay on the saddlehorn. He leaned forward and laid his own calloused paw on that white hand.

"When can I see you again?"

She raised her eyes and looked directly at him. Her hand trembled under his, but she didn't move it.

"It's not wise. You know that."

"Wisest thing I ever did."

"The first time I saw you, I thought you were an honorable man. I hope I'm right. You could misunderstand what I'm going to say."

"Say it. I'll understand."

"I'm friendless and have been ever since I came to the Rigdens three years back. You look like you could be a good friend. I ride each day and I go to the Bishop's Rock. Do you know it?"

He nodded.

"When I can," he told her, "I'll be there."

He lifted her hand to his lips. He had never done a thing like that to a woman before and he was surprised at himself. He was a kiss-'em-and-bed-'em man with no preliminary nonsense. Suddenly with a woman he knew caution. This was one in a million. She would come only to a man she trusted. He knew that instinctively.

She let her hand lie in his for a moment before she gently released it.

"Thank you," she said. "You've done me a lot of good. I had forgotten there were men like you."

"Don't fool yourself," he said, "I'm a roughneck like the rest."

She smiled.

"You're a roughneck," she agreed, "but not like the rest."

When she rode away from him down the steep southward trail, he watched her go with a feeling of misgiving, hating the fact that she was going back to the man Rigden's house. When she reached the flat, she turned and waved and then lifting her horse into a brisk trot was suddenly lost in timber. He turned his horse and went slowly home.

When he reached there, he felt that he was a man he had never been before. Some of the wildness was gone. It was as if he had been suddenly sobered by a draught of fresh air. He was like a man awakened. The whole world looked different.

He went to Ruiz and Pete at the corral.

They sat on the top rail of the fence and listened to him.

"There's trouble coming," he told them, "real trouble and there's most likely a hangrope for the man that mixes in it. I only pay you wages and I can't expect you to face that for what I pay you. If you don't want any part of it, I'll pay you and you can light a shuck and no hard feelin's."

They sat and looked at him. Then they looked at each other.

Ruiz said: "*Por Dios*, I have been in plenty trouble in my life. Why should I run from it? Tell me, I would like to know. I have ridden for many brands, but I never left one because some hombre wanted to part me from it. I stay, patron."

"How about you, Pete?"

The Minneconjou gave an Indian shrug; he stuck his fingers out close together and stiff in McAllister's direction as if he were supplicating him.

"What is this question?" he demanded. "Should a man run from a fight? Does he run from good food or a strong woman? Then why should he run from a fight? That is what man is here on earth for — food, women and fighting. I stay, I think."

McAllister was not surprised. He did not thank them, but accepted their loyalty as due to a brand. All right, he told them, if there was going to be a fight, then they must get rid of the stock that they had penned. They were a valuable investment and the money was needed. Therefore, Ruiz and Pete would set out now with the remuda of broken horses for the fort. The major who was buying the horses at Fort Stewart expected them. The two horse-breakers didn't need any second bidding. While McAllister rustled up supplies for them, they caught up a saddle-horse each and a pack horse to carry the supplies. While McAllister gathered the grub together he worried a little. Horses weren't easy animals to trail and it was a three day journey to the fort. But, he argued, his two men were both good with horses, even though three riders would have been better. But he couldn't afford to have this place completely denuded of men. Besides somebody had to go into town and fetch in the supplies that would be necessary if the range-war reached the bench.

He lugged the supplies outside and started to load the pack horse. Ruiz and the Indian were as excited as school-kids at the prospect of the trip. McAllister told them to take their side arms and they fetched them from the house. Then they forked their horses and were off with McAllister ordering them to keep moving. He wanted them back quickly. He rode with them as far as the saddle that acted as a pass in the hills to the northern plain and then he turned back.

The house felt very deserted when he reached it. Ruiz and Pete had been company and for the last few days the corrals had been filled with horses. Now there was only himself and the saddle-stock. He checked on their feed and water and worked a little on the coyote dun. Then it was dusk and he sat on the stoop and thought about Rose Carmichael. He knew that Hardy Rigden or no Hardy Rigden, he would marry her.

6

THE following day, he hitched the two stout wagon horses to the light wagon and with half his savings in his pockets, he headed for town. He came down from the bench in a dawn that was full of birdsong and felt fine. He didn't feel so fine when he stopped off at Whittaker's place to say hello and found it deserted. The door was open and he went in and saw that the settler had moved out lock, stock and barrel. He didn't waste his time here, though the stillness of the place filled him with foreboding. He got onto the wagon seat and picked up the lines, thinking that at least Whittaker had gotten out alive. He drove on the mile to the next house in some trepidation, not knowing what to expect. Here the Olsen brothers bached together. They ran a shirt-tail cow-outfit and were reputed to subsist on hunting game and other men's cows. They were a tough pair of second generation Swedes, not overly bright, but they didn't frighten easily.

He found them both at home with the doors and windows barred.

They let him in and offered him breakfast.

They were the long and the short of it, these two. Lief, the elder, was a tall gangling man with a shaggy fair beard. Eric, the younger, was short and bald. They lived rough and they were as fierce against the outside world as two wolverines. But they welcomed McAllister as one on their side of the fence. They knew that it had been him who had found Holley and taken his body into town. They had heard also of his fight with Rigden, for the tale had run across the country like wild-fire.

McAllister could have wished for better allies, but at least they had some spunk. He told them that he was going into town and asked them if they wanted for anything. They wanted ammunition, they told him, but they lacked money.

"Pay me in beef," he told them with a grin, "whoever's it is."

They were not amused and they nodded solemn agreement. He left them with a handshake, telling them that if it became untenable down here, they could join him up on the bench. They told him that they had not received a personal warning from the Association yet, but they knew they were included in the general threat.

McAllister drove on to town.

He reached Lennox without any incident and went straight to Bright's store for his supplies. He was surprised to see the sedate sheriff wearing a holstered gun over his apron.

"Why the gun?" he asked.

Bright sighed and spread his hands.

"I must be everything," he said. "No deputies. How can a man keep order in a wild country like this without deputies?"

McAllister said: "You asked me once before and I said 'no'. Now I'm sayin' 'yes'."

Bright looked pleased.

"I guess you've been threatened," he suggested.

"You guess right. A badge wouldn't hurt under the circumstances."

Zane Bright's face split in a sad smile. He administered the oath then and there, took a badge from his pocket and pinned it in McAllister's vest as if he kept a store of the things for would-be deputies. People in the store turned and stared.

McAllister said: "Can we talk some place?"

"Sure, come on out back."

They walked through the store to Bright's tiny office at the rear. The sheriff lit a cigar and McAllister filled and lit his pipe.

"Could you use a drink?"

"Thanks."

The sad sheriff poured for the pair of them and they drank. The hard liquor felt good to McAllister who didn't taste much of it these days.

"I'm glad you come into town, McAllister. How long you been here?"

"I come straight to you."

"Then you didn't notice our population has risen a mite." McAllister shook his head. "Around twenty fellers come into town on the train this mornin'. All the same kind. They all carried guns and they all looked like a man's life didn't matter a red cent to 'em."

"You done anything about them?"

Bright shrugged his helplessness.

"What can I do about them? They haven't broken any law. If they did, I don't know what I could do on my lonesome. I'd have a try maybe, but it would only get me dead I shouldn't wonder."

"Where're they at now?"

"Drinkin' it up down at the saloon with Rigden's riders and the Association man, Church, just like they're old buddies."

It stood out a mile. Bright and

McAllister both knew it. But neither could prove a thing.

"They've got saddles, but no horses. But they'll get horses. Bet your life on that."

"Rigden in town?"

"I ain't seen him."

McAllister finished his drink. He stood up.

"You have any ideas how we play this?" he asked.

"Nary a one except by ear," Bright told him. "I don't mind tellin' you I feel a whole heap better now you have that badge on your vest. All I know is there's trouble comin' and it'll most likely come up your end of the country. If any of them settlers'll stand an' fight, I'd make every man jack of 'em a deputy."

"They say you're a nester sheriff."

Angrily, Bright said: "I ain't nobody's sheriff. I'm the law. The Association and the big cattle companies think they're above the law. They ain't as they'll see if they cross me."

"They'll cross you all right. If they do, will you fight?"

The sheriff heaved himself out of his chair. He looked straight at McAllister.

"You think I'm just a soft storekeeper," he said, "an' you're entitled to your opinion. One day I'll show you different."

McAllister said softly: "I think you will too." He nodded to the sheriff and left the store. On the sidewalk he paused and saw a large wagon coming in from the east. Behind it trailed a buggy and several horsemen flanked it. One of these was Hardy Rigden. They came slowly along the street until they stopped at the store. Rigden and the riders got down and the cattleman stepped up on the sidewalk. He saw McAllister, paused for a moment to stare wordlessly at McAllister without an expression on his face and then walked into the store. McAllister turned on his heel and walked down the street.

When he reached the saloon, he

didn't need to look inside to tell that it was full. The noise that came from there was enough. He opened the door and went in. There were some townspeople in there and a few riders from ranches around town, but the place had been taken over by Bright's twenty men from off the train.

There was no missing them.

Bright had been right — they were all the same kind. The type of men that McAllister had known all his life, the kind that had tamed the frontier, who had hunted buffalo, broken the law and sold their guns to the law in endless frontier towns. They were, he had to admit, his own kind.

The only difference between them now was that they all wore guns and McAllister did not. The only weapon that he had with him was the Henry repeater out there on the wagon.

The first man he saw when he stepped up to the bar was one he knew. This was Andy Osgood. He had been a deputy in Abilene, wanted for murder in Texas and had finished up as a guard in the Santa Fé railroad trouble on one side or the other.

He stood shoulder to shoulder with Bill Kilgore who had seen service with McAllister and Church against the Apache and who had roistered and fought from one end of the frontier to the other. Osgood was a beefy man with red hair and beard, a dead shot with a pistol and hell on women and horses. Kilgore was a tall saturnine man, poisonous in drink and as quick with his gun as his temper.

Osgood saw McAllister first. He let out a roar.

"Look who's here."

Kilgore turned and saw McAllister. His dark face lit up. The two of them rushed at the big man and started pounding him on the back, punching him and shaking him by the hand as excitedly as two schoolboys. McAllister was genuinely pleased to see them. He pounded back and laughed with them, but one part of his mind stayed wary.

A little man howled out of the crowd.

McAllister's hand met his and they shook. The little man laughed, delighted. This was Harry Sandoz who had been everything in the west from a stage-guard, through nursing cows to robbing banks. The governor of Colorado had given him a free pardon for certain depredations carried out in that territory and it was said that the little man was comparatively honest now, though his gun was still for hire for the classier type of venture. Like this one, McAllister thought. While he laughed and joked with them all, a cold feeling of dread went down his spine. He was with his peers here and they greatly outnumbered him. He would have taken on any one or maybe two single-handed, but twenty of them was altogether too much for a man to stomach.

Kilgore, Osgood and Sandoz were heaved aside and McAllister had to raise his eyes to look up at Buff

Thompson with whom he had ridden almost as many trails as he had with Joe Church.

He and Buff shook and McAllister winced as the massive hand gripped his.

Buff said: "Good to know you're with us, Rem."

A cold voice cut in.

"He ain't with us, boys."

McAllister turned to Joe Church standing there.

"Ain't with us?" Buff said. "Hell, an' was countin' on havin' a deputy on our side."

"Deputy?"

Church was surprised. He had not seen the badge McAllister wore till now. He looked a little taken aback.

"Since when?" he asked.

"Does it matter?" McAllister said. "It's there."

Osgood asked: "You mean you ain't in on this, Rem?" He sounded really disappointed.

Before McAllister could reply, Church

said: "I told you boys that the sheriff in these parts is a nester sheriff. McAllister's his deputy. Add it up for yourselves.

There was complete silence in the big room. They all looked at him.

Kilgore said: "Is that right, Rem?"

McAllister looked around him and he knew that before very long, if he didn't watch himself, he was going to be in a fight.

"Joe could of put it a different way, boys. He could have said I run a horse ranch and I mind my own business, I don't steal cows an' I'm a deputy of the legally-appointed sheriff of this county. Does that put me on one side or the other?"

Joe Church cleared his throat and the sound was loud in the stillness.

"You can't talk your way out of this, Rem," he said.

McAllister thought: *This is Joe's chance to whittle me down. He knows I can be his main opposition and he's going to stop me right here.*

"What's there to talk my way out of, Joe?" McAllister asked.

Kilgore demanded: "Put it plain, man. Are you for us or against us?"

McAllister said: "I walk into a saloon and I see a whole bunch of my old friends, fellers I've rid with. That's all I know. You mean you're all here for a purpose? You mean you've all come in from the outside for a purpose?"

Osgood grinned briefly and not in a pleasant manner.

"We're agents of the Cattlemen's Association. We're all accredited range detectives."

McAllister said: "You mean you're all hired guns come to frighten men off land they've all got legal claim to." He could feel the cold rage rising in him and he knew that he was one step from real trouble. He measured the distance to the door and saw that there were at least a half-dozen men between him and it. He was a dead duck.

"That don't give them a legal right to steal association beef," Kilgore said.

"If there was anything to prove, the sheriff's office would look after it," McAllister said. "There's no argument to turn you boys back. You've hired your guns to clear this country of farmers and little cattlemen. Sure there're some cow thieves among 'em. Just as there're cow thieves among the big 'uns. Tell me the big man that didn't make his start with a running iron and a wide and careless loop."

Somebody pushed himself to the front of the crowd. He was little more than a boy and he was drunk. McAllister didn't know him, but he had seen him drunk in here before with Willy Toff and Strange.

"You callin' my father a thief?" he demanded fiercely.

"Who're you?" McAllister asked.

"I'm Brett Rigden."

The anger flared in McAllister. He never knew why the sight of this drunken boy was like a spur to his rage.

"All right," he said softly, "I'm callin'

your father a thief. An' more. You tell me why he run out of Texas."

The boy took an uncertain step forward. His face was suffused and his eyes wild.

"That's a damned lie," he shouted. "My father wasn't ever run out of anyplace. Clear this saddle-bum outa here, men."

Joe Church put a hand to restrain him, but he knocked the hand aside.

"The boy's drunk," McAllister said.

"Liar."

Another voice joined in.

"I say you're a liar too, mister."

McAllister turned his head and saw Willy Toff. The boy had a sneering smile on his face. He was evening the score for the humiliation McAllister had offered him on the street. His hand rested on the butt of his gun.

McAllister considered the situation.

He knew that he dare not back down. Just as surely, he knew that he dare not take any action or he was finished. What to do, then?

The door of the saloon swung open. Heads turned. Rigden walked in with several of his riders.

Now there's no escape, McAllister thought. He was either going to take the beating of his life or he was going to get killed. But he did not think that they would kill him here in town. They would wait for him on some lonely trail.

McAllister said: "Your boy's drunk, Rigden. Take him home before he gets himself into trouble."

Rigden looked around at the assembled men and laughed.

"Looks to me like you're the one in trouble, McAllister," he said.

"He called you a thief, pa," Brett said.

Rigden's eyes levelled down to McAllister's. He walked slowly toward him. "Did he now?" he said softly. McAllister waited. Here it came.

Rigden turned to the men near him.

"Take him," he said.

The men started forward. McAllister

went into action. He charged without any warning on Willy Toff as the boy heaved his gun from leather. The gun was knocked from his hand and fell to the floor with a clatter. Somebody kicked McAllister's legs from under him and he would have fallen if he had not caught hold of the bar. he pushed himself around and found himself face to face with Osgood who drove a punch for his belly. McAllister caught the fist in his hand and drove his knee up into his former partner's crotch. Osgood made a keening sound and went out of the fight.

They swarmed over him.

He smashed a fist into a jaw, ducked under a swinging right and moved his head out of the way of a flashing gun-barrel. The heavy weapon hit his shoulder and jarred him right down to the wrist. He hurled himself at the mass of men in front of him, driving his shoulder into the chest of a man and knocking him from his feet, swinging on another and burying his fist in a belly up to the elbow.

Then his legs went from under him again and he crashed down on a table. He hit the floor and tried to roll away from the booted feet, but they came just the same from all directions. The toe of one caught him on the temple and he almost passed out. He tried to get to his feet, but somebody hit him over the head with a gun-barrel and he went down again.

He came to when somebody threw a jug of water into his face.

Shaking his head, he sat up.

He heard Rigden's voice.

"Get him to his feet."

They hauled him up and held him. He tried to focus his eyes and saw Rigden's face dimly in front of him. Rigden stood there watching him till his sight was cleared.

"Can you see me clearly, McAllister?"

"Yeah."

Slowly Rigden drew his gun and for a moment McAllister thought that the man was going to shoot him, but that was not Rigden's intention.

"Right now I'm goin' to mark you, McAllister, so you'll remember me. Later on I'm goin' to kill you."

McAllister braced himself. He tried to free himself from the men who held him, but they were too strong for him. They were Joe Church and Kilgore.

Rigden hit him in the face with the barrel of the gun, using the foresight to good purpose and McAllister felt the warm flow of blood down his face. The man hit him again and again and he sagged in the strong arms of the men who held him. Rigden came in for a final blow. McAllister summoned every ounce of his remaining strength and kicked out with his right foot. It was a bad aim, but he managed to kick the man on a knee. With a howl of rage and pain, Rigden fell to the floor. Eager hands helped him up and he stood and raged, holding the agony on his knee.

"Throw him out into the street," he shouted. "Throw him out before I kill him."

They lugged McAllister to the door and pitched him across the sidewalk onto the street. He raised his face from the dust, coughing on it and made an attempt to rise. But he passed out and fell flat. They walked back into the saloon for another drink.

McAllister lay on the narrow cot at the rear of Bright's store.

"They've gone," the sheriff told him.

McAllister sat up and found that he ached from head to foot. The boys had lost none of their thoroughness over the years. They could still nearly beat a man to death without killing him. Bright had patched up the worst of his cuts, but it would be days before he could sit a horse without wincing. He stood up and the room turned over a couple of times.

"A damn good start to being a deputy," he said. "I shouldn't of gone near that saloon."

"What's done is done," Bright said. "We have to put our mind to what those men are going to do next."

McAllister said: "I don't think there's much doubt what they're goin' to do. What we want to know is when and where? I'd best get home and start work."

"You're sure you feel up to it?"

"I have a feelin' I've got to be or I'm a dead man."

He put on his hat and Bright walked with him to the street. The sheriff said: "Don't forget if you can swear some good men in, do so."

"I'll remember."

He climbed aboard the wagon, now loaded up with supplies Bright's man had put aboard, and moved off down the street. The town was quiet now, but as he passed the saloon he saw Rigden seated on the sidewalk smoking a cigar. The man gave him a sardonic grin as he passed.

McAllister promised himself that Rigden would smile on the other side of his ugly face before he was done. Every jolt of the wagon gave McAllister pain, every rut the wheels passed over reminded him of his defeat.

Night fell before he had gone a few miles from town and he drove warily with the rifle at his side. He wouldn't put it past Rigden to make an early move in the game, but nothing happened. He reached home about midnight, unhitched the horses, put them into the corral and fell into his bunk to rest his aching body.

He didn't feel much better when he awoke the following morning, but he was able to go about his chores, caring for his stock. But he did little else. Once the stock was cared for, he sat in his rocker smoking and watching the skyline for movement or dust. The day passed uneventfully.

The second day, he felt a good deal better although his head still felt as if it had been torn off and been put back again by unskilful hands. However, he saddled the dun horse and rode south with a vague hope that he would meet the girl on her ride. He reached Bishop's Rock in mid-morning. The young horse had given him a good ride and shown that it had learned its lessons well. But he was not sorry to leave the saddle and rest his aching bones among the rocks.

He had not been there half an hour when he saw dust to the south. He stood up expectantly and saw after a while with some excitement that it was the girl. She rode in among the rocks and dismounted lithely before he could help her. This disappointed him slightly for he had been looking forward to getting his hands on her.

"Good morning," she said as if to indicate that they were polite strangers.

"Mornin'."

He loosened the cinches on her mount for her and they strolled into the shade of the timber at the foot of the rock. It was a balmy morning with the sun warm in a clear sky. They sat and she propped herself against the bole of a tree.

"I hoped you'd be here," she told him.

"That sounds promising at least."

"I have some news for you."

She told him then of the men that had arrived at the Rigden place. She knew little about them except that they had been hired by the Cattlemen's Association. She told him what she knew, but added little to what he knew already. The men slept in a large barn on her brother-in-law's place. Daily they practised with their fire arms. She did not know what move they were about to make. Then abruptly, she said: "You have been fighting again." It was an accusation as she inspected the raw marks on his face.

He smiled crookedly at her.

"It wasn't a fight. It was a slaughter. This time friend Hardy had the big battalions on his side. I don't have to tell you who won."

There was concern in her fine eyes.

"Were you hurt badly?"

"No ribs broken, but they left their

mark. Rigden also told me that the next time we met he'd kill me. War's declared."

"Wouldn't it be wise," she said, "simply to saddle your horse and ride out of the country. Nobody would blame you."

"Nobody but myself. No, that'd be no solution. I came to this country with my mind made up to sink roots. I've sunk some and it'll take a big heave to uproot me. I'm going to survive to have the best horse ranch in the territory. I'm goin' to build a fine house and install a beautiful wife in it. Preferably one who can cook."

"I hope we're not going to start that again."

It was a rebuke, but when he stretched out a hand, she took it in hers with hesitation.

"You have thought about it?" he said.

She nodded.

"When a woman reaches my age, she thinks about any proposal."

"What kind of persuasion do you need?" he asked, pulling a little on her hand. She resisted. He persisted. Finally he had her near him and he managed to kiss her gently on her cheek. It was the gentleness that surprised her and made her turn to look at him. She had thought him a man of violent passion. This gave him the opportunity to kiss her on the mouth. She tried very feebly to pull away, but his mouth won. She turned and relaxed into his arms and his hunger touched that which lay dormant in her.

When he pulled his head away from her, he smiled and said: "Even better than I could have dreamed."

She disengaged herself and started to tidy her hair, for her hat had fallen off and her hair was disarrayed. He sat entranced, watching her.

She gave a wry and shy smile.

"I must confess that you can do something well beside fighting, Mr. McAllister."

He stood up and looked at the

distant horizon. He ached from head to foot still from the beating he had taken, but he had never felt better in his life. He turned to her.

"Rose," he said, "we could make a go of it, you an' me. I can see you in my house with my kids. My God, if you can cook as well, why it's a hundred per cent certainty."

She laughed and the sound of the laugh was like music to him.

"I can cook," she said.

"Then that does it. You must marry me."

She sobered quickly.

"I'm no child," she said. "I'm set in my ways. There's Hardy and this war that's coming."

"Does any of this stand in our way if we let it? Or is it just me? Do you feel I'm not the man for you?"

She looked at the ground.

"It's not that I feel you're not the man for me," she said softly.

"Rose," he said. "I ain't foolin'. There's a future here for the pair of us. All we have to do is ride into town and have the judge marry us."

"I know. You're not the only one to feel an impulse. I've been careful and fastidious all my life with men and now suddenly I feel I want to act purely by instinct because I know my instinct is right. But there's more to it than that. I'm not a young girl and I know there are other things to be considered."

"What other things?"

"My sister."

"Where does she come into this?"

"I went to live with her because she finds life with Hardy unbearable. We both thought that my being there would help. Not that it does, much. But we're together and that helps some."

"She has her sons."

"They follow the father."

He dropped on one knee beside her and took her hands in his.

"You have to think of yourself," he told her.

"If you were in my shoes, you wouldn't just walk out."

He knew that was true enough and there was nothing he could say.

"You can't be tellin' me there's never going to be any hope," he said. "Heck, I ain't takin' that, girl."

"There's always hope. Something will work out. Maybe when this fight's over."

"Everything will be just the same only maybe Hardy will be lordin' it over more land and more men."

The rest of their time there together was not all unhappy. She lay in his arms under the trees with the soft sound of their horses munching on the grass nearby and he knew again with complete freshness, as if he had not known it before, that she was the right woman for him. Their very flesh complemented each other.

At last, however, it was time for her to go. They led the horses to the pool under the trees and watered them. Then they embraced and kissed again and he helped her into the saddle.

"I won't be here for several days,"

he said. He thought. "If you can get away, let's say four days from now. All right?"

"All right," she said. "I'll count the days."

He voiced a doubt that had been in his mind all along.

"Hardy," he said, "does he trouble you any?"

She touched his face with her hand.

"Don't you fret," she told him. "I can handle Hardy."

She bent from the saddle and kissed him. Then she turned her horse and rode away. He hated to see her go, but he forked his horse and headed for home. From the tops of ridges they halted their horses and waved. Then he set the dun for home and hit a fast gait.

On the trail he met two wagons travelling together. He stopped and talked with the drivers. There were women and children along and the wagons were loaded with their worldly possessions. They were two families:

The Harkisons and the Broadribs, both farming families. The men were scared and McAllister didn't blame them. They had plenty to be scared of. They knew the gunmen had ridden into the territory and were at Rigden's place and they had been delivered warnings. It was time to go. They had left crops standing in the fields and just pulled out. The women were in tears when they told their tale.

"Don't go further than town," McAllister said. "Camp outside town by the creek. Maybe this'll be over inside a week."

"We don't have no hope, McAllister," Broadrib said. He was a big, slow-moving farmer of English stock. "But we'll be around town for maybe a few days. We have the wagon to sell. We're goin' back east by train if we have enough money for the fare."

McAllister rode on depressed. Both farmers would have been good men to have along, but a married man and father owed it to his woman and kids to stay alive. A man couldn't fight on those terms. His only hope was in the Olsens and other men like them. Which meant that he would have to rely on the less savoury of his neighbours. He grinned wryly. He would have to make this fight with what were probably genuine rustlers on his side. Might well be that they were the real fighting kind.

He turned the dun aside from the trail and went west heading for the Olsen place, but when he got there he found the door wide and the place deserted. There were no horses in the corral and the wagon had gone. So the Olsens had pulled out too.

He went on further west into the poorer country at the foot of the hills where the Wellmans had their place. They raised a few cows and the women had a few chickens pecking around the door. The Wellmans were two brothers, Jeff and Lee, and a cousin, Morgan. They were surly truculent men and it was as much as they could do to wish a neighbor a good day. But they were tough and he reckoned they wouldn't knuckle under to the Rigdens of this world easily. As fighting men they would not be the best disciplined, but they would fight, McAllister banked on that.

He found Morgan in the corral working a colt. The man was strangely pleased to see McAllister. He noticed the badge on the big man's vest right off.

With a grin, he said: "So the law's come to these parts."

McAllister grinned back. He stepped down from the saddle and they talked. No, Morgan said, his cousins were not around. They were back in the hills gathering cows. Had they been warned by the Association? The man nodded. Yeah, they'd been warned all right. That's for why they were gathering cows. McAllister asked him if they were thinking of moving out of the country.

"That's what that blow-hard Rigden'd like us to do," the man said. "But we ain't movin' for him nor no association. We're stickin'."

"I've got grass a-plenty up on my bench," McAllister told him. "You could do worse than drive your cows up there. They'd put some tallow on up there and you could make a stand from the high ground."

The man stared at him, thinking.

"Maybe you got something there," he said. "I'll tell the boys. But we ain't runnin', you kin bet on that."

"What about the women and kids?"

"We kin allus hide 'em back in the hills if'n the weather holds off."

"They could use my house."

The man would think about it and talk it over with the 'boys'. Having to be satisfied with that, McAllister headed for home. He passed Rickards place on the way and found the one-room shack deserted. There were no horses in the corral. It looked like Rigden wouldn't have much to use his gunmen on. The country was emptying out fast.

7

HE noticed the cows as soon as he hit the bench. There were a half-dozen of them scattered on the rich grass and they wore the ear-marks and the Double O connected of the Olsen brand. So he didn't experience much surprise when he rode in to find Lief and Eric sitting on his stoop drinking whiskey.

They greeted him with a little cheer and offered him some of his own liquor. Their wagon was drawn up in the yard and he noticed that it was well stocked with supplies. What interested him was that Carl Rickard was there with them.

He was a small bow-legged man with the evil reputation of a horse-thief. He was alive now, so it was said, on account of the superior quality of his horse flesh and the speed of his gun. He had a passion for horses, particularly other people's. For which reason McAllister considered he needed a close watch kept on him. He was a man of about thirty-five, small, wiry and tough. McAllister liked him and found him quiet but genial. He was in fact the most genial man going. It was said that he could shoot a man to death and smile pleasantly over it.

He got to his feet now and came forward to shake McAllister by the hand. He noticed the badge and remarked on it. Laughing softly, he said: "Looks like I'm going to have the law on my side for a change."

It appeared that all three men had come up onto the bench to stay until either the trouble blew over or they beat it. It was the considered opinion of all of them that they would have to beat it.

McAllister got himself a cup from which to drink his whiskey and they there and then formed a council of war. They decided, much to McAllister's surprise, that they needed a leader and they wished McAllister to assume that position. This was something coming from three such wild and unruly men. They finished the bottle of whiskey and discussed weapons and methods. The Olsens possessed each a Colt six-gun and shared an old Remington single-shot rifle. Rickard had a colt revolver and a Spencer repeating carbine. McAllister had his old Remington .44 back in the house, his Henry repeater and the two new rifles he had bought. With some pride he fetched them from the house and presented one each to the Olsen brothers. He had, he told them, enough ammunition for an army and supplies for several months. He was ready for a siege and would not be surprised if there was one.

But, he told them, the fight would not necessarily be from this house. The three of them hadn't come up to defend his house when they could not stay and defend their own. Most likely they would all have to take to the hills before they were done. Caches of food and ammunition would have to be made in the hills and they would have to turn many of the horses loose and construct a hidden pen for some for immediate use.

They talked it over this way and that and looking around at each other all tacitly agreed that if any four men could make a fight they they needn't be ashamed of, they could.

They all retired to rest that night, not dissatisfied with the work of the day. The Olsen boys took Ruiz and Pete's bunks in the house and Rickard, ready to outflank any attack on the house, made himself comfortable in the hay in the barn.

Rose Carmichael rode her mare into the yard of the big house and at once became conscious that she was exposed to the gaze of the men outside the barn. With their eyes, they stripped her naked and she knew it. Flushing red, she handed her lines to one of Rigden's riders and hurried into the house.

The first person she met in the hall was Hardy Rigden himself, the last person she wanted to meet. He blocked her way into the house with his legs spread apart.

"Where you been?" he demanded, glaring at her from under the fierce bushy gray of his eyebrows.

She pulled up short, startled.

"Riding," she told him.

"Where?"

"No place in particular," she said. "Just riding."

"No more riding," he said, "Not till I say."

She drew herself up indignantly.

"I beg your pardon," she snapped.

"You heard me. I told you there'll be no more ridin' out till I say. There's things goin' on I won't have my women mixin' in."

"I'll have you know, Hardy," she said loudly, trying to keep the fear of the man from her voice, "that I'm not one of your women and that I'll ride out when and where I please."

Over his shoulder she saw the tall Burt standing there, looking as morose as usual. She could expect no help from him.

Rigden took a pace toward her and before she could avoid it, he had caught her by the wrist and hauled her toward him. Her face was forced close to his and she smelled the whiskey on his breath.

"While you're under my roof an' eatin' my food," he told her through his yellow teeth, "you'll do like I say, hear?"

"Let me go."

"When I'm good an' ready."

He was hurting her, but her pride would not allow her to admit it. Burt took a hesitant step forward and said: "Pa."

Over his shoulder, Hardy Rigden asked: "Yeah?"

For a moment, Burt looked as though he would say something, but instead he simply said: "Nothin'."

"Then shut up." Then to the girl, Rigden said: "I know where you been, girl. You been cattin' it around after that McAllister. You know that man's an enemy of this house, but just the same you — "

"He isn't an enemy of this house," she said. "He's a man who had the courage to stand up to *you*. You can't bear that, can you?"

He flung her away from him so that she collided with the wall.

"I never wanted you here," he said. "You're no damn good. But you do like I say or you'll be sorry."

He tramped to the door leading to the yard and stormed out onto the stoop. Burt and his young aunt looked at each other.

"I'm sorry, Rose," the boy said.

She rubbed her sore wrist.

"You're sorry," she said. "But you never did a thing. Why don't you get a mind of your own, Burt?"

"Heck," he said, shrugging his

shoulders. "You know the way things are. You know Pa."

"I know you're a man grown now and you've got to choose your own path and walk it. You're different from Brett and your father, Burt. Why don't you get out while you can?"

"I can't. Why don't you?"

"There's Margaret."

Burt nodded. "Remember she's my mother," he said.

"Oh," she said, "what's the use?" and walked past him and went up the stairs. He stared after her for a moment, his prematurely heavy face troubled, then he walked slowly out into the yard.

8

THERE was a full moon. The horses were saddled and the men stood by them, waiting for Joe Church.

He was in the office with Rigden and his two sons.

"Come on, Joe," Rigden was saying, "have a drink. A man always fights better with a drink under his belt."

Church accepted the drink and looked at the three men facing him, the father and two sons, the two younger men so very different. Burt, the elder, not having touched a drink watched the others out of dull cowlike eyes. Appearances were deceptive and, though Church had never seen him in action, he had heard from the men of the crew that this one was a heller in a fight. Didn't know when he was beaten. He threw his slowness off when he faced action.

Brett, the younger, was altogether different. Fair where the other was dark, quick where he was slow and now half drunk while the other was cold sober. And Church knew which one he would choose in a fight. He knew both boys were coming along with him. Their baptism of fire, the father called it. But he would rather have left the young one at home. When one like that got to shooting, he didn't know when to stop. Church was an old campaigner. If a man had to be killed, he would do it without a qualm, but he didn't like promiscuous killing and he had a feeling in his water that this one was a killer. The eyes and their wicked meanness told their story.

"Well, we'll be gettin' along, Mr. Rigden," he said. "Tonight and tomorrow should see it finished. There's just one thing."

"What?"

"These two boys of yours. They do

like I say. No privileges and no cryin' 'boss's son'."

Rigden looked angry, then he laughed. "You don't know my boys," he said and clapped them both on the back with his great hands. "Trained to take orders. An' fightin's in their blood."

"Let's hope there's no fightin'. A show of force should do it tonight. Maybe a barn burned down."

"For Crissake," Brett said. "You mean the bastards won't fight?"

"You see?" Rigden shouted with delight. "A chip off the old block. Rarin' for a fight. Now you simmer down, son, and do what Joe here says. This ain't playin' at cowboys an' Injuns. This is for real. You clear that neck of the woods of nesters and your work'll be done. Nothin' fancy. Just clear 'em out. An' your ole pa'll be proud."

"We'll be back here by sunset tomorrow at the latest," Church said. "Then the men get paid and we clear out of the country before the hue an' cry."

"Understood," Rigden said.

He shook hands with all three of them and wished them luck. When they walked out into the yard, he came out onto the stoop to see them off.

They tramped through the dust to their horses and Church gave the order to mount up. Feet went into stirrup irons and leather creaked as men heaved themselves aboard. Bridle chains gave off their faint music. Church led the way slowly away from the house and the men followed.

Rigden stayed where he was, listening to the sound of the horses walking away into the night. He nodded and smiled to himself, satisfied. This time he was getting his violent way and it was sanctioned by his fellows. Riding away there on his business were hired guns of the Association and riders from every outfit in this part of the country. There must be nearly fifty men there. An invincible army and all they had to move on were a pack of hungry nesters who were rustling his cattle.

He took a cigar from his pocket, lit it and puffing he walked into the house.

Just inside the door he met his wife.

"I suppose," she said, "that you're satisfied now. You sent my two sons maybe to their deaths."

For him, he spoke mildly.

"*My* sons," he said, and pushed past her into the house.

It was Carl Rickard who spotted the flames of the fire on the other side of the valley. It was he who had been elected as the first watch on the edge of the shelf near the trail that led down into the valley. He and Lief Olsen were camped out there. Lief was snoring in his blankets and the horse-thief was perched up in the rocks with his rifle in his hands. He sighted the twinkle of the fire and knew that it was the Olsen place that was burning.

He slid down the rock he was on and strolled to the sleeping Swede whom he woke with his toe. The big man came grumbling awake.

"What the hell?"

"Come an' look, Olsen."

The Swede swore a round oath, heaved himself out of his blankets and tramped morosely after the smaller man. Rickard led the way back to the rocks, climbed up with the other heaving after him and pointed across the dark valley.

"Goddammit," Lief said, "that's our place."

Another twinkling light caught Rickard's sharp eye.

"An' that's my place," he said. He didn't feel much because one house was to him much the same as any other. But it angered him that a man could do that without him putting lead through his guts.

"This has gotta mean," Olsen said, "that they'll come this way tonight."

"It means too that they've split up. Those two houses're four-five miles apart."

"Could be there's a third party

headed this way."

"Let's ride."

They scrambled down the rocks, rolled their blankets and threw saddles on their picketed horses. They went up the bench at a flat gallop not caring about the risk they took in the dark. Both were relieved that they had changed their sleeping arrangements at the whim of McAllister in the middle of the night. They thundered into the yard and awoke the sleepers with their yells. McAllister and Eric Olsen appeared showing that they had been sleeping in their boots.

Rickard told them that his and the Olsen places were burning.

"Son of a bitch," Eric said.

McAllister said: "Most likely they're headed this way. Joe Church will want me finished. And so will Rigden."

"What do we do?" Lief asked.

"We'll make a fight for the house," McAllister told them. "But we don't fight too hard for it. No house is worth a man's life. We'll use this one as a bait. We want it to look like there's only me here. Let's get your wagon out of sight down the draw yonder."

They cleared the wagon from the yard and took some of the horses into the barn so that they would not be immediately obvious. Then McAllister told the Olsens to take up their positions in the house, but on no account to show that there were two rifles in there until Rickard fired from the barn where he would be hidden.

"Where will you be?" Rickard asked.

"I'm goin' to range down the bench to sight them when they come in. My warning will be a coyote howl like this." He demonstrated to them. "Then I'm going to take them from up in the rocks. That means that you'll have them outflanked if they're between you an' the house, I'll have 'em outflanked if they're between me an' the barn."

McAllister went into the house and changed his boots for a pair of Cheyenne moccasins. The Olsens took up their positions in the house after McAllister had shown them the gully that would help them escape under cover and take them to the draw if things got too hot in the house. Rickard would be in a less envious position in the barn. Once he was in there he would be hard put to escape if he wanted to.

McAllister saw the horse-thief settled down in the barn-loft and then he started out through the darkness toward the edge of the bench, loping through the dark night, stopping every now and then to listen.

He took up a position under cover of rock and waited patiently until about one hour and a half from dawn. Then he heard men leading their horses up the steep trail from the valley. He got to his feet and ran hard straight across the bench toward his house.

9

JOE CHURCH stood by his horse letting it blow after the steep climb up to the bench from the valley below. He could hear the soft murmur of the men's voices. He admitted that he would have liked to smoke, but he dare not for there might be a rifle out there in the darkness.

He was up against McAllister and he knew the man. Every rider there knew him, all seven of them, and there wasn't a man there who didn't wonder if they had enough men there to settle the big man's hash. That wasn't true — there was one man there who thought that it was going to be a walk over. His name was Brett Rigden. And he was at that moment enjoying what was currently his fondest dream: he leaned against his saddle and pictured himself cornering a cowering McAllister and shooting him dead. That would show the old man that there were two Rigdens who knew what was what.

Burt Rigden was there too. He exhibited no feelings. He looked his usual morose self, but he was feeling taut and nervous. He wasn't a coward, but he was made of flesh and blood and he was old enough and imaginative enough to know what a well-placed bullet would do to a man.

The rest were seasoned fighters, but all of them knew tension. All of them knew that if they didn't catch McAllister with his pants down there was going to be one hell of a fight.

Harry Sandoz, Kilgore and Osgood centered on Church. Kilgore had his cheek full of a wad of chewing tobacco. It was the next best thing to smoking.

He said: "You know the place, Joe, an' we know the man. How do we play this?"

"We ride along nice and easy to make as little noise as possible," Church told them. "Then we go in on foot and should reach the house in the dawn. He has to come out for a leak like any other man. Then we take him."

Sandoz said: "If'n we can. For my money, he'll be shooting first."

"Yeah," Osgood put in, "let's face it. We have to kill him. McAllister ain't goin' to be took."

Church nodded agreement. There was cold regret in his voice.

"He'll have to be killed most likely. I can't see any other way."

Osgood said: "Let's git on an' finish it."

They walked to their horses and stepped into the saddle. Church led the way north, walking his horse. He did so for nearly an hour, picturing the lay of the land to himself in his mind, planning his moves, knowing from memory where he would place his men.

When he halted, he gathered the men to him and told them that they had to be silent. To the two Rigden boys, he said: "He's a heller. Watch what the others do if you don't know, but keep your heads down or you'll get them shot off."

Brett laughed.

Church didn't say anything. He led the way on through the darkness. They followed him, toting their rifles and their boxes of ammunition. They knew that they might be emptying them before this chore was finished. All of them, except two had seen McAllister in action.

After a while, Church halted and started whispering to the men giving them their instructions. They started fading away into the darkness, taking up positions all around the house. Kilgore headed for the corner of the barn, Osgood and another man wormed their way silently around back, Sandoz hunkered down on the side of the corral nearest the house from which he could shoot through the windows and the door. Church and another man took up positions in the corral on the edge of the yard and settled down. Already the cold fingers of dawn were edging across the sky. The men shivered in the cold a little and breathed on their fingers to warm them for shooting.

They waited.

They were still waiting when the sun was up and every detail of the place was plain to them.

McAllister crouched up in his rocks and watched the men below. He could see Osgood and a companion to the rear of the house. His best target was Kilgore behind the barn. He could see the tip of a man's hat on the edge of the corral near the house. He knew that there were other men out of sight on the other side of the barn. He didn't want to have to kill his former partner. He didn't want to have to kill anybody, but he knew that men would be dying down there mighty soon. Kilgore would most likely be the first to go.

Silence lay heavily over the whole scene. McAllister guessed that the men below were waiting for him to walk out of the door into the yard. Already their patience was beginning to wear thin.

But the silence dragged on.

McAllister lay with his cheek against the stock of the Henry thinking of how he had ridden with those men, how strange it was that they and he who had ridden the same trails and lived the same life had now taken such divergent ways. What made a man change. Once he too, like them, had lived by the gun. But now he had hoped that he had put guns away for good. Times had changed and so had he, but those men down there had not changed. They had got it in them to give up the old ways. But here they were once again united on the same trail with guns in their hands. In the West it seemed that all questions had to end in violence. Everything was settled finally with guns. The solution of every question was in gunsmoke.

The silence was broken.

Somebody was shouting.

"McAllister . . . McAllister . . ."

No reply came from the house.

"McAllister . . ."

It sounded like it was Joe Church shouting. So he was here after all. He and Joe would be swapping shots. Perhaps it was inevitable.

"McAllister . . . we know you're in there. Throw out your guns and come on out with your hands up. The whole place is surrounded. You don't stand a chance."

A single shot came from the house.

Another short silence followed.

This was blasted asunder by every rifle around the place opening up. McAllister saw hats pop into view as men raised themselves from cover to shoot. Bullets ripped through the oil-cloth cover of his windows, they slammed into the door and the shutters over the two windows he could see. They rained on the house at all angles. But only one rifle replied from the house as McAllister had ordered.

McAllister thought: *This is where it really starts and finishes.*

Acute sadness and depression settled on him and he levered the first round into the breech.

Kilgore was at the corner of the barn, firing steadily through the ripped window covering, giving the supposed one man inside a taste of what he could expect if he didn't give up.

Deliberately, McAllister shot him through the back.

He watched him fall to the ground and kick a couple of times and drove a shot through his head. That was the end of Kilgore with whom he had laughed and drunk.

He watched Osgood turn and gaze up at the height, alarm in every line of his body and at that moment, the second rifle in the house opened up and Rickard started shooting from the barn.

McAllister levered and shot three times at Osgood and the man with him and saw them scuttling away to the gully to get away from the shots from above.

Men were shouting down below there.

A man ran into view from behind the barn, running away wildly from the shots which were so unexpected. McAllister swung the Henry and drove a shot through one of his legs. The man tripped and went down, rolling over and over and McAllister heard his yell of pain and fright clearly.

Shots were hammering out wildly now.

A man ran across the corral. It looked like Harry Sandoz. A shot got him either from the house or the corral. He went down. He didn't move after he hit the dust. The horses in the corral were going crazy at the sound of the gunfire. They bunched and streamed frantically around and around.

McAllister could see nothing to shoot at, though he did catch sight of the tips of two hats as the men in the gully tried to get out of the fight. Osgood was a man who knew when he was licked. The rifle up above in the rocks had settled the conclusion of the fight for him.

McAllister stood up, clambered out of the rocks and started slowly down the hillside, the rifle held ready, his eyes alert.

A gun started booming in the confines of the barn. A man ran from the outer edge of the corral and he saw that it was Joe Church and in that moment he saw the first wisp of smoke from the barn. Two more men ran into sight from behind the barn. Dirt spouts showed near them as hidden rifles tried for them.

McAllister broke into a run.

He turned toward the house so that he would have the barn between himself and the fleeing men. When he reached the corner of the barn, the men in the house had flung open the door and jumped into the yard, shouting and firing after the fugitives.

As he went past them, McAllister

shouted to them: "There's two in the gully at the rear."

He took his rifle in his left hand and drew his pistol, knowing that if there was another man in the barn beside Rickard there was going to be some close work.

As he ran though the wide open door of the barn, the heat hit him. There was a sheet of flame barring his way. He stopped and yelled Rickard's name.

"Here."

It was one short word, but it was shouted by a man driven by desperation.

McAllister holstered the Remington and dropped the Henry in the dirt and, with an arm across his face, plunged through the flame. It was a line of straw that had caught and he was soon through it. Beyond the place was filled with smoke. The main bulk of hay had just caught.

Another faint cry from his left reached him and turning he saw Rickard lying on the hay, his face convulsed with pain. McAllister went to him and the man told him: "I got it in the leg."

McAllister bent and lifted the small man in his arms and stumbled hastily down the barn, going through the spreading flames. A second later he was in the yard, rolling the wounded man in the dust and beating the flames out with his hands. Rickard lay there smoking and groaning. McAllister beat at his own clothes.

All the while, lead sang through the air. McAllister looked up to see rifle smoke coming from a ridge at about one hundred and fifty yards distance.

He said to Eric: "Get Rickard in the house. Leif, let's go an' clear these jaspers out of there."

"What about the barn?"

"There's no saving it."

He retrieved his Henry from the dust and ran for the cover of a grassy hummock. He started firing at the ridge. It didn't take many minutes for him to estimate that there were three men behind it. One of them he reckoned was Joe Church.

Lief Olsen was down behind some stone to the right, firing away steadily. McAllister reckoned they had reached a stalemate. Joe wouldn't budge from up ahead there and didn't seem strong enough to come back and finish it. McAllister had a good look around. There was a wounded man in the corral and a dead man behind the barn. Between himself and the barn lay a wounded man. He looked like the young drunk who had braced him in the saloon before he had taken his beating. Young Brett Rigden.

McAllister called over to Lief.

"Hold your fire."

The Swede gave him a sign to show that he had heard.

"Joe . . . can you hear me, Joe?"

The cry came back.

"I hear you."

"Let's talk."

"All right. Halfway without your guns."

McAllister laid down his rifle and put his pistol beside it. He stood up and said to Lief, "Cover me. He tries anything, you kill him, hear?"

"Keno."

Joe Church stood up and they walked slowly toward each other.

When they met halfway, they took a good look at each other. Both were black with burned powder. Church had taken a bullet along one cheek bone and it looked like it had hurt him plenty. The blood was running down into his shirt collar. He sagged a little.

McAllister said: "Neither of us can win, Joe. We can swop shots all day."

Church nodded.

"Looks that way. But I have some men alive behind the house."

"They run for it when I opened up."

"They could come back."

"Not Osgood. He's tough, but he likes a winning fight. You thought you'd caught me here on my lonesome, didn't you?"

Church nodded.

McAllister said: "I have one wounded. You have two wounded and one dead."

"Kilgore?"

"Yeh. We'll pull back into the house and you can come and collect your two. I'll bury Kilgore."

"All right. But this ain't the end of it, Rem. I'll be back and next it'll be with an army."

McAllister smiled.

"That's what you'll need, Joe — an army. But if I was you, I'd cut my losses an' pull out. You ain't goin' to get yourself nothin' but grief outa this."

"I never backed down in my life."

"Then more fool you. You stay here till we pull back into the house. You stay in sight all the time. One of you gets out of sight and the others get shot. Hear?"

Church nodded.

McAllister turned and walked back. He passed Lief Olsen and told him: "Pull back into the house." The Swede stood up and gazed suspiciously at Church for a moment then started walking backward to the house. McAllister went into the house and saw that Eric had put Rickard on one of the bunks. The horse-thief looked as if he had passed out. When Lief came into the house, McAllister barred the door and told him to watch the rear of the place. He went to a window and opened the shutter. This gave him a clear view of the yard and beyond. He watched and saw another man join Church. They walked toward the house. Nobody else appeared. Either McAllister had been mistaken and there had only been two men behind the ridge or they were up to something.

They went first to Brett Rigden and stood talking together looking down at him. Then they heaved him on his feet and the man with Church put him over one shoulder and walked staggeringly away with him. Church went into the corral and did the same with Sandoz. McAllister watched them out of sight.

That left the two men to the rear of the house.

He stood up and walked over to Rickard.

The horse-thief grinned when he saw him.

"It ain't much," he said. "Lead went right through my laig. Give me a week an' I'll be ridin'. Thanks for dragging me outa the fire."

McAllister shrugged and called to Lief.

"Let's go winkle them two outa the gully."

They hefted their rifles and went.

10

JOE CHURCH was feeling bitter. At the start of the fight there had been in him a certain reluctance to fight McAllister and to kill him. But now that he had tasted defeat, there was none. He knew that he would go back there and settle what had now become a personal matter with him. McAllister had shamed him in front of their peers. He would get enough men to finish this and go back there. He'd burn that damned house to the ground, pick up his pay and go.

As he came to the head of the steep trail leading down from the bench he stopped and looked out over the valley, eyeing the billowing smoke of the burning homes coldly. They were sacrificial fires to the bull god. The new was being destroyed in flame so that the old could live. Inside a couple of days this whole corner of the territory would be clean of nesters and the cattle would come in in their thousands.

He looked around at the men with him.

Sandoz, shot through the side, leaned forward precariously in his saddle, hanging on for dear life, knowing that if he didn't make it to a doctor pretty soon, he'd be a dead man. But not a word of complaint came from him nor ever would. It was a part of his iron code.

Young Brett Rigden rode white-faced beside his brother. Every now and again a low moan would issue from his lips. He had a bullet through the fleshy part of his left calf and they had fixed him a tourniquet so that he would not bleed to death. He looked sick and sorry for himself. Burt rode with him, not saying a word, looking as morose as ever. Church thought the boy had done well in his first taste of burned powder.

Bringing up the rear were Osgood

and Rates, both oldtimers and both accepting their temporary defeat stoically. They would keep on coming till things looked right for the kill. They'd be riding back again with Church.

They went slowly down the steep trail, taking it easy because of the wounded men and when they hit the flat they wheeled left along the valley, riding beside the water of the creek after they had slaked their thirst and allowed the horses to drink. An hour before noon they came to the camp of the small army.

Jeff Wellman, the nester, watched them come down the trail from the bench from the timber across the creek. He waited till they were out of sight and hurried back to where the two wagons were parked. His brother Lee and his cousin Morgan were there with the women. They had halted at dawn in the cover of the timber when they had heard gunfire on the bench.

Now Jeff told them: "Church and his men just rode down the valley. They looked like they took a whuppin'. Let's git on."

They crossed the creek without much difficulty beyond Jeff falling in and getting a wetting. The kids laughed a lot at that until he angrily came from the water and yelled for them to shut their noise. But his brother and cousin laughed too and there wasn't much he could do about that.

When it came to the steep trail up onto the bench they found themselves with a problem because the wagons were heavily laden with all their treasures of furniture from the houses. They had to take them up one at a time with the two teams hitched.

While they did it, Lee rode a saddle-horse down valley and scouted for any sight of the gunmen, nervously, his rifle in his hands. He spotted nothing but some distant horsemen riding south at a fair pace. He reckoned they were a bunch of the gunman riding back into camp after a successful burning. When he rode back, he found that the two wagons were up and were rolling along the bench toward McAllister's place. He then took up a position at the head of the trail and watched the valley for any sign of danger.

The wagons were spotted from the house long before they saw it. McAllister rode out to greet them and he seemed pretty pleased they had come. By the time they reached the house, Lee rode in to join them and after they had all eaten a good meal, the men had a council of war in the yard. They hunkered down on their heels and listened for a while as McAllister drew a plan of the valley and the bench and the hills beyond with a stick in the dust.

The Wellmans' coming in, he told them, had made a considerable difference to them. But they didn't make them strong by a long chalk and they brought the additional difficulty of women and children. The men discussed that this way and that, all agreeing that it wouldn't be safe to have them at the house. If the weather stayed clear, they must move them back into the hills for safety. But they didn't like the look of the weather; the sky was starting to cloud over and they all thought it looked like it was going to rain cats and dogs.

They went over their stock of food and agreed that it should be held in common, as should ammunition. So they unloaded the food from the wagons and carried it into the house. Then they made sure there was plenty of water in the place. They filled every container they could lay their hands on and got them inside. The kids played around the yard as if there was no danger just around the corner. The women sat on the stoop and talked together in low voices. To McAllister they took the situation with incredible calm. There was Netta, Jeff's wife, a big hearty woman with red apple cheeks and it was rumored great skill with a rifle.

Her sister-in-law was Mary, Lee's wife and she was a small quiet woman with a tight mouth and a determined look in her eyes. There were some eight children ranging from fifteen down to two. McAllister wondered what the hell they would do if an attack came while they were all here.

When the water and the food had been stored in the house, the men talked again.

Rickard hobbled from the house with a stick and joined them.

"What I got on my mind," he told them, "is the other way onto the bench. They could come that way."

McAllister nodded.

"They sure could. An' Joe Church knows it because he rode that way the other day when he was here."

"Which way's that?" Morgan Wellman wanted to know.

McAllister told him as he pointed north-east: "The saddle up there. It'd take them a day or more to get around from the valley, but there's nothin' to stop them doin' it."

It was decided that Lief Olsen should ride to the saddle and camp up there, watching, while his brother Eric went to the trail up from the valley to the bench and did the same. They obtained supplies from the house and saddled their horses. They rode out in the middle of the afternoon, saying that if they heard the sound of shots, they'd come a-running.

After that the Wellmans helped McAllister knock down the remains of the smoldering barn so that it would not afford too much protection for the attackers. That done it was nearly dark. Just before dusk gathered in on them, Pete and Ruiz rode in from the north saying that they had met Lief on the way. McAllister had never been more pleased to see two men in his life. Now his little army was starting to be something.

After dark, everyone retired to sleep for they would need all they could get. But there was an alarm in the middle of the night when Eric Olsen rode in and said that he had heard the sound of horsemen coming up the trail from the valley. Everyone stood by their arms and everybody packed into the house.

Not long after, in the full light of the moon that came sailing out of a bank of dark cloud, they saw two riders come to the edge of the yard.

"Hello, the house."

McAllister thought there was something familiar about the voice. He stepped onto the stoop with his rifle held ready.

"Who's this?" he demanded.

"Harrison," came back the reply. "I've got Broadrib with me."

A babble of voices greeted this declaration. These were the two men that McAllister had met moving into town with their families. The two men came forward, dismounted and told their tales.

They had reached town and camped with a view to moving on, but they had heard rumors that there was a gathering of settlers up on the bench. Thinking that their women and children would be safe camped on the edge of town, they had decided to come back and make a fight for their land. They'd had trouble down in the valley when they'd run into a scout belonging to the gunmen. They had swopped shots with him and run for it. But neither were hit and they were here safe and sound. The women found them food, Lief rode back to keep his vigil and once more everybody sought their blankets.

McAllister lay on the stoop, head leaned back in his clasped hands and thought about his strategy and tactics. He thought a long time, decided what he would do and went to sleep with a comparatively easy mind.

In the night it rained hard.

McAllister awoke, watched the rain for a little while and thought that put a stop to the women and kids going off into the hills.

11

JOE CHURCH sat in the firelight and watched the circle of faces around him.

He thought: *By God, if I can't do it with these men, I can never do it.*

He still smarted bitterly from his defeat at the hands of McAllister. He had brooded silently ever since he had ridden down from the bench. He would go back and settle with that bastard if it was the last thing he did.

"This is what we'll do," he said. "We'll start from here at dawn."

"Dawn," Osgood said, whittling on a stick, "hell, that's when we want to hit 'em."

Church turned on him coldly.

"Do you *want* men to die, Osgood?" he demanded.

"Hell, no."

"Then let 'em see us in force. Let

'em watch us walk our horses slowly along the bench and know what's going to hit 'em. That'll give 'em an hour maybe to see what they're in for."

A murmur went around the circle.

"We'll ride up there nice and easy after a good night's sleep and a breakfast under our belts and we'll let them see what they can expect. Picture it, boys. Maybe four men in that shack and they watch forty men come along that bench. Put yourselves in their boots."

A man laughed.

Smiling at the prospect, Osgood said: "Do it your way, Joe. Was I in their boots I'd come out with hands up."

"And with your pants messed," a man shouted.

A loud laugh went up.

Joe Church said: "Hit the sack, boys. You'll need your sleep."

They stirred themselves, searching out their bed-rolls, some of them relieved the way Church meant to do it, saving bloodshed.

They hadn't been in their blankets a couple of hours when the heavens fell. It rained hard all night and scarcely a man had a night's sleep. The earth beneath them turned to mud and the cook in the morning was hard put to get his fire going. Men cursed each other, bleary-eyed and morose. However, an hour after dawn, the sun came through and they started to steam in its warmth. But they were far from a happy crew as they saddled up and stepped into wet saddles. They cursed each other, they cursed Joe Church and they cursed McAllister, hoping now that it would come to shooting and they could kill him. Forty edgy men lined out from the camp and headed for the bench.

They reached the bench mid-morning and scrambled up the steep trail. By this time the morning was hot and they felt the tension ease a little in the heat.

Donovan, the man who had brought the horses in on the train for the little army, was the first to see the wagon track and to suspect that maybe they were riding into more than they had expected. They all halted and gazed at the tracks.

Joe Church said: "So a couple of wagons came up from the valley. They had women and children with them most likely. How's that goin' to help McAllister?"

They rode on. The sky started clouding over and before very long, it frowned down on them blackly. Miserably, the riders waited for the rain to come. But it held off and a keen wind blew along the bench, scudding the clouds before it.

McAllister watched the large bunch of horsemen come slowly along the bench and he would have been a liar to himself if he had not admitted that the sight depressed him. He knew that Joe Church would come back with reinforcements, but he never guessed that he would be here so soon or with so many. It was just as well that he had taken the precautions. Since dawn, he and the men had been digging. They had hacked rifle pits out of the earth east and west of the house in positions that would cover the north and south approaches and which should help to overcome the attacking force's outflanking of the house. It might also draw some of the fire away from the women and the children.

The westerly pit had been dug between the house and the creek. Here the water was shallow and Church could have brought men in from that direction to fire on the house from the cover of the creek bank. The one to the east was high on the slopes that led up to the first untidy spread of rocks. Its weakness was that it could be overfired from anybody that could get up in the rocks. McAllister wished he had enough men to cover that eventuality.

He was in the eastern pit with a fair view of the northern part of the bench either way from his position. With him he had the phlegmatic Broadrib, a steady man and a good shot. Harkison and Lief Olsen were in the western pit covering the creek crossing. Eric Olsen, the three Wellmans, the wounded Rickard and the women and children were in the house.

Not for the first time, McAllister wondered if he had done the right thing to split his forces. Certainly, if he had put everybody in the house they would have presented a tightly packed target. He prayed that the women and children would come through unscathed. Maybe if he talked with Joe, Church would allow them to walk out. Not even a cold man such as he could want to make war on women and kids.

He watched the riders pull up just beyond good rifle-shot.

They stayed where they were in a long line stretching a quarter of the way across the bench, their horses knee-deep in the grass, watching the house. Horses' heads tossed, men shifted in their saddles. Absolute calm prevailed for a moment in time under the lowering skies.

Slowly a rider detached himself from the line and came forward at a walk. Slowly as he came closer he revealed himself as Joe Church. He headed for the house and halted on the edge of the yard. He didn't look up the hill in McAllister's direction and McAllister reckoned that the man was unaware of the rifle-pit's existence. He sat his horse quietly for a moment, then hailed the house. He sounded absolutely calm.

The door of the house opened and Eric Olsen, rifle in hand, shoulders hunched, walked across the yard toward him, halting a dozen yards from him. They talked for a while, Olsen turned and tramped back to the house again. The door slammed behind him. Church stayed where he was, motionless. The minutes passed and McAllister would like to have known what was being said inside. He thought most likely that Eric was trying to persuade the women to go and they were refusing to be parted from their men folk. McAllister would expect such a reaction from them. Finally, Eric came out onto the stoop and shouted: "You go to hell, Church."

Joe Church rose in his stirrups and yelled back: "Don't be a fool, Olsen. You'll all be killed."

"That's a chance we'll have to take."

"Think again, man. There's women and children in this."

Eric levered a round into the breech of his rifle and bawled out: "You git the hell outa here or I'll drill you."

Church didn't say anything more. He turned his horse and rode slowly back to the line of riders. When he reached them he spoke to those nearest him, then he turned in the saddle and stared for a long time at the house. It seemed a long time before he started shouting orders and pointing in various directions.

McAllister watched the men in the center dismounting. They lay down in the long grass and almost disappeared from view. The men on the flanks stayed mounted and started to move forward, going out east and west. Those in the west trotted their horses along the edges of the creek and disappeared into timber. Those in the east rode their horses up the gradual slope of the bench to gain the high ground above the house.

McAllister watched these.

"We don't let them reach the rocks," he told Broadrib.

The man said: "They're in range now. Do we shoot?"

McAllister reckoned that there were eight men in the bunch. A formidable opposition for two men, but the gunmen were in the open and the two defenders were hidden in the rifle pit. That evened up their chances. But immediately they revealed their position, the fun would start.

McAllister levered a round into the breech of the Henry.

"Come nice an' close," he whispered. "Nice an' close."

As if they were obeying him the riders swung along the edge of the rocks and started an arc of a movement to come out directly above the house. They were south and slightly above the men in the trench.

McAllister glanced at the ground below. The men on the bench itself were showing themselves as they ran a few paces and flung themselves down in the cover of the grass, always working nearer to the house. The men on the other side of the creek were not in sight.

He looked at the riders near at hand. They were maybe one hundred and fifty yards away.

"Now," he said.

He would start the ball. He and Broadrib rested their elbows on the lip of the trench and sighted on the two leading riders.

McAllister said: "Take the man to the left if you can, kill him. Don't monkey around."

Broadrib fired.

McAllister's shot followed so closely that the two sounds were one.

Broadrib's man dropped his rifle and fell forward onto the neck of his horse. He clung there for a moment with his arms clasping the horse's neck, then slipped to the ground. The horse shied sideways and started cropping the grass. McAllister's man was turning in the saddle when he fired. The heavy bullet caught him and drove him back over the rump of his animal. The horse started pitching wildly down the slope of the bench, bouncing the man free, his arms and legs as lifeless as a puppet's.

For a moment, it was as if every man taking part in the drama froze to the spot. Heads had popped up from the grass to see what had happened. Rifle-fire broke out from the house.

McAllister and Broadrib saw nothing but the men immediately opposed to them. They levered and fired, levered and fired, until they lost count of the shots they had expended, pouring lead into the little bunch of horsemen. Men and horses screamed, animals pitched wildly, men turned and spurred away, one made for the rocks, flung himself from his horse and dove into cover. In a few seconds it seemed it was all over on the east side of the bench.

McAllister and his companion stopped firing.

They looked at each other.

McAllister saw that the man was sick to his stomach. At least three men had been killed out there. He didn't feel too good himself. But there was more to be done yet. It hadn't started.

He looked east and saw horsemen leaping their animals into the ford of the creek, water plummeting out from the horses' hoofs. Rifle fire came flatly from the trench over there. A man was torn from the saddle and dumped into the water with a great splash, a horse went down, men were frantically turning their horses, trying to get away from the devastating fire. Slowly a dead body floated away downstream, face down in the water, arms and legs outspread.

Then all was still.

Black powder smoke drifted on the light breeze.

McAllister and Broadrib started to reload. McAllister stood, watching the east end of the bench. There was one man already in the rocks up there. Soon the rest of the riders would join him. That would make a possible five up there. While it was daylight, the rifle-pit would have to be held.

McAllister said: "I'm goin' up into the rocks. Cover me."

"Don't be a fool," Broadrib told him. "You've got a hundred yards to cover. They'll get you from below."

"Cover me," McAllister repeated.

He threw his rifle over the end of the trench, heaved himself up onto the surface of the ground, picked up the rifle and started to run.

It was tough going from the start,

going uphill all the way over rough ground. And at once he was spotted from below. The rifles opened up and the lead whined angrily in the air. He heard it plough into the dirt at his plodding feet or sing by to strike rock and ricochet with the buzz of a furious bee. Once something plucked at his sleeve and every step he took the flesh of his back crept in the expectancy of a bullet. But with heaving chest and complaining lungs he reached the rocks and flung himself among them.

His first thought was: *Has the man in the rocks seen me?*

Once again the rifle fire down below died away. He peered out from his cover and saw the forms of the attackers creeping forward through the grass. Broadrib opened up on them from his vantage point.

McAllister started to work his way south through the rocks. Two hundred paces to his left towered the first shoulder of the mountain, dwarfing the antlike men below it.

He crawled a short way into deeper cover and then started south slowly, eyes everywhere, rifle held ready. His nerves were strung taut and he would have fired at anything that moved. As he went slowly forward it started to rain again, a gentle fine rain that scarcely made a whisper of sound. The rifles down below started up again.

He must have moved forward cautiously like that for five minutes before the shot came.

12

IT tore his hat from his head.
It came from his left and it had sounded pretty close. He flung himself down, hurt himself on the hard rock and rolled. Even as he did so, a second shot came and drove dust and stone chips up into his face.

He scrambled desperately to get away then, staggering to his feet for a couple of yards and flinging himself down again. Another shot winged past his ear.

He got himself behind a giant boulder. The marksman made one more try. The shot hit the surface of the rock and whirred away into space.

Shaking and cursing in both fear and anger mixed, he feared to even put his head out of over.

He backed up around the rock,

found a way into a thicket of brush and started pushing his way through. He reckoned he made so much noise that the other man must have heard him. He did. When the shot came, it tore through the brush a few inches above his head. He got down on his hands and knees and crawled. His spurs and his rifle caught in everything they could and he found that even in the coolness of the day he was sweating profusely.

He got through the brush and found nothing but open space. The rifleman spotted him and sent a shot that hummed so closely by his head that he ducked down and went back the way he had come. By this time he was becoming a little frantic. God damn the man, he had him pinned down and helpless.

There was only one thing to do. Go back.

So he backed up, keeping the giant rock between himself and the man who wanted him dead. He went back a hundred paces and then found good cover. At once he started toward the mountain to the east, going as fast and as silently as he knew how. When he thought he had gone far enough, he started working his way south so that he would come up on the man's right.

No sooner had he reached a point which he thought to be about a hundred feet from the man's former position, than he was startled to find himself looking directly at him as he advanced in a crouching position toward the giant rock behind which McAllister had hidden.

He was debating whether to take the man prisoner or shoot him down in cold blood, when he heard a scrabble of rocks to the south and, turning his head, saw three men emerge from the rocks. They were on foot. McAllister dropped into cover. The man he was stalking heard the others and turned to face them.

"There's one up ahead," he called.

They ran up to him and stood with him staring at the rock at which he was pointing. They were separated from it by some fifty yards of open ground.

On slightly higher ground as he was, McAllister had them all cold. He could have killed two of them with no trouble at all. He should have done. He knew that. There were women and children below in the house depending on him. But he could not.

He cursed himself silently for his softness and sang out to them.

"Drop your guns."

They turned as one man. Eight eyes were suddenly wide with astonishment and apprehension. Two of them, he reckoned, were hard-cases, but the other two were just working cowhands. One man was hidden half behind another.

"Drop 'em."

The rifles clattered to the ground. The four of them stood there reminding him of naughty children caught in the act.

"Now unbuckle your gun belts real

easy. But first spread out a little so I can see you."

The man who was half-hidden from him made his move. He was fast. His gun appeared past the arm of the man in front of him and he fired two shots almost as one. That was his fault — he fired too fast. One struck the rock in front of McAllister's face, the second almost parted the big man's hair.

McAllister fired.

The shot hit the man covering the man with the gun. He threw up his hands and walked slowly away from the others, aimlessly.

The man with the gun fired again while the remaining two flung themselves flat on the ground. But the pistoleer had too small a target to shoot at. He was a sitting duck himself. McAllister fired again. The man's right leg seemed to fly out from under him and he fell hard to his right side. He floundered for a moment like a landed fish before he cried out: "Don't kill me."

McAllister got to his feet and walked

forward. He hefted the Henry in his left hand and drew the Remington.

The man he had shot first was sitting up and holding his side.

"Christ, man," he said, "you've killed me. I'll bleed to death."

The two men who had flung themselves to the ground got shakily to their feet.

"The gunbelts," McAllister reminded them.

They took off their gunbelts and dropped them to the ground. The two wounded men made no move.

"You too," McAllister told them and sullenly they obeyed. He watched them. They both looked in shock. "Step back from the guns."

The man with a wound in his side said: "We can't walk."

"Then crawl," McAllister told him.

They both crawled. McAllister turned to the two men who were unharmed.

"Pick these two up and get outa here," he said. "I see either of you around this neck of the woods again and you're dead men, hear?"

They nodded and picked up their fallen comrades. McAllister stood and watched them staggering away into the rocks. He holstered the Remington and threw the discarded guns as far as he could. The ammunition belts he slung over his own shoulders. He tramped back the way he had come, suddenly exhausted as though he hadn't had a wink of sleep in days. He reckoned that was the way tension and excitement took some men.

When he reached the edge of the rocks, he surveyed the scene below him. It looked as though the battle had not progressed since he had left it. To the west the attackers had settled down on the far side of the creek and were swopping shots with the men in the trench over there. The attackers on the flat had ventured no nearer the house. The firing from the house itself was steady but not intense. Broadrib in his trench was not shooting. In fact, McAllister could not see him at all. Apprehension for the man hit him. He shouted his name and received no answer.

He broke from cover and started for the rifle-pit. He covered a dozen yards before the men on the flat below sighted him and turned their rifles on him. Again the air was full of flying lead, but again the range was difficult for them and they were shooting uphill, never an easy thing to do. He leapt into the trench and landed on top of Broadrib.

The man was lying on his back in the mud with the rain playing on his face. His hat had come off and revealed an ugly wound that began at his temple on the left side and ran along the side of his head. His eyes were closed.

McAllister leaned his rifle up against the side of the trench and took off the man's bandanna, tying it tightly around the head to stop the flow of blood. Broadrib opened his eyes.

"My Gawd," he said. "My head."

"It's a graze, that's all," McAllister told him.

"A graze. Hell, it feels like I had my haid blown off." He tried to sit up but couldn't make it.

"Lie there. I'll get you down to the house after dark."

"I'm all right," the man said and succeeded in his second effort to sit up. He looked terrible, pale and with blood down one side of his face.

It was dusk.

McAllister was tired to the bone and chilled by the rain.

"Come on," he said, "let's go."

Broadrib grumbled and got to his feet, leaning against the side of the trench. McAllister climbed out of the trench and gave the man a hand out.

"Can you walk?"

"Sure. They didn't hit me in the laig."

They started down the hill together, going as quietly as possible. When they neared the house and before McAllister could sing out a shot came from the dark building. McAllister yelled his name then. A voice bade him come ahead and several shots came through the darkness from along the bench showing that the attackers were still there and had heard him. When he reached the stoop, supporting Broadrib, the door opened and they stepped inside.

"Light a lamp," McAllister said.

A lucifer scratched and the faces of the men, women, and children there sprang into relief. The lamp was lit and McAllister looked around.

It looked as though a tornado had hit the inside of the house. Flying lead had ripped the place apart. It seemed that not a square foot of the place had gone untouched. China was shattered, wooden sides to bunks were splintered, mud chinks between the logs had been broken away.

"My God," he said.

It seemed impossible that the people inside could have survived. It turned out that Ruiz had been hit in the arm, one of the Wellman boys had been torn by a ricochet in the fatty part of his belly and a child had been grazed on the face by a bullet. So far nobody had been killed.

The women started at once to patch Broadrib up. While they were at it, the men began to talk, keeping watch at the shutters all the while. During the talk, they were hailed from outside and Harkison and Lief Olsen came in from the western pit. They looked like men who had been through a harrowing experience.

"No good stayin' there," Lief said. "They could swarm all over us in the dark."

Which was true enough, McAllister thought. But without the outposts, it meant that the gunmen could swarm all over the house.

From the southern window, Pete called: "Something movin' out there. Near the barn."

McAllister joined him and stared

through the rifle slit into the darkness. One of the defenders should be out there scouting around. If the attackers found that it was safe to move near the house, it might be too late by dawn to do anything about it. He looked around at the faces of the women and children and saw the strain showing there.

Suddenly rifle fire started outside.

Inside the house, somebody reached out and extinguished the light. Lead slammed with a booming sound into the planks of the shutters, it ripped through the house and struck the opposite wall. A woman screamed with a short sharp note and a man shouted: "Get down." The women and kids got down on the floor and the men blundered through the pitch darkness to the windows.

The firing was kept up for maybe ten minutes. Suddenly it stopped and in the silence that followed, McAllister asked: "Anybody hit?"

A woman's voice said: "I am."

Jeff Wellman said: "It's my wife. I'll see to her."

They heard him crawl across the floor. The man and the woman murmured together.

McAllister made up his mind. *I'm going out there.* It was a crazy thing to do, but it was no crazier than staying here and letting women and kids get shot.

"I could talk to Joe Church," he said. "He'd let the women and children walk outa here."

Jeff said: "Netta, say something. Netta, you're goin' to be all right, honey."

No sound came from the big woman.

A child said: "Maw, maw." The girl began to cry. "Maw's kilt."

A man swore softly in the darkness.

Jeff's voice came: "She's daid."

They were all silent, a hopelessness and a dread that was indescribable coming over them.

McAllister came off his knees by the window.

"I'll see Church," he said. "He's got to let the kids go."

The voice of Lee Wellman's wife, Mary, came from the darkness. "Me an' the kids ain't movin' from here. Our man stays, we do."

They waited. McAllister knew that the woman couldn't be moved to alter her mind. Outside the gunman started throwing lead at the house again, but the firing was not so intense as before. McAllister knew that the guns were close in now and that when dawn came, the place would be rushed.

He was going out there.

"I'm goin' out," he said.

Lee Wellman said: "It ain't no use talkin' with them devils."

McAllister laughed unpleasantly.

"I ain't goin' to talk with 'em. I'm goin' to kill some of 'em."

A man moved blunderingly in the darkness and knocked over an article of furniture. He walked across the room and from near McAllister came Jeff Wellman's voice.

"I'll go with you."

"No sense in that, Jeff," McAllister told him. "We'd only be shootin' at each other in the dark. If I go alone I know if anythin' moves it's one of them."

"Then let me go alone."

"No. You have kids to think of."

A man said: "He's right, Jeff."

Jeff moaned softly to himself in his grief.

McAllister said: "Open the door, Jeff, and have the men hold their fire either till dawn or till you hear me come back. I don't want one of your bullets up my butt."

Jeff said: "All right."

There came the sound of the bar on the door being lifted. McAllister leaned his rifle against the wall and eased his Remington in its holster. His hand touched the hilt of his knife to check that it was in place. The dark was the time for the knife.

Jeff opened the door and McAllister saw that it was slightly lighter outside the house than in. He closed his eyes for a moment and then opened them so that he could see better. He got down on all fours and crawled out onto the stoop. As the door shut softly behind him a bullet slammed dully into it.

13

McALLISTER rolled off the stoop and lay still, listening. He could guess where the man nearest to him lay. The only good cover offered was that of the nearly destroyed barn. The next best close to the house was the rather doubtful protection of the corral rails. Beyond that was the rifle-pit to the west of the house between the corral and the creek. It was his guess that both trenches were now occupied by the gunmen. There would also be men waiting near the barn and in the corral. The restlessness of the horses told him that the latter was correct.

He reckoned that the first move he could make was to belly between the ruined barn and the upslope rifle-pit to the east. If he chose his path well he would be out of earshot of both positions. The start of the maneuver offered the most danger. Then it would be plain going until he got near the men on the other side of the barn. That would be the time of the greatest danger.

He started crawling.

He covered several yards and stopped to listen. Nothing.

He covered a dozen yards and stopped again.

Somewhere off to his right he heard the faint sound of a gun coming to full cock. He relaxed against the ground, lying very still. He was working on instinct alone now for he could see very little. From uphill he heard a soft murmur and knew that he was right and gunmen now occupied the rifle-pit up the slope of the bench.

He went on again, crawling directly south and then stopping when he thought that he was opposite the southern end of the wrecked barn. Then he turned to the right and went in the direction of the creek.

Now he moved with even greater caution, inching his way along on his belly, stopping frequently to listen. He tried to move now so that even he could not hear his own movements. He had all the time in the world, he tried to tell himself, and his life and maybe the lives of the people in his house depended on his skill.

Instinct halted him.

The faintest of sounds reached his ears and he lay still trying to interpret it.

Gradually, the truth came home to him.

He was lying near a man. The sound he could hear was heavy breathing.

He closed his eyes for a full minute. When he opened them, he thought that he could make out the dim form of a man not six feet away from him. From maybe twenty yards away, he heard the soft murmur of voices. Two men joked grimly together in the darkness.

Then, startlingly, a rifle opened up

not a dozen feet to his right. He heard the bullets slamming into the house. It was the muzzle flash that showed him the exact position of the man near him. A man kneeling, crouched up. McAllister caught the general shape of the hat and the hunched shoulders and then the impression was gone. He reached down and eased the knife from its sheath resting on his right buttock. He thought for a cold moment of what he was about to do and knew that it was not going to be pleasant. To plunge cold steel into a man unaware in the dark was not easy, nor would it be a pleasant thing to live with in the future. If he was alive to live with anything in the future.

Raising himself slightly, he got his right foot under him.

Now, his mind told him and he rose silently to his feet, lunging forward and raising his right arm for the blow.

He halted and drove down with all his strength, feeling the hilt of the weapon hit flesh and knowing that the blade had penetrated entirely.

The man screamed piercingly.

The night seemed to come apart with the sound. McAllister heaved on the knife and got it free. There was a loud explosion near at hand and he knew that the man had triggered off his belt-gun in his death throes.

A man nearby shouted.

The stabbed man came erect and turned, yelling loudly, deafeningly. McAllister swung his right arm and lunged at the dark bulk. Again the knife went home and the man clutched at him. McAllister batted the gripping hand aside and the man went down.

McAllister heard him thrashing about and then he lay still.

A man called: "That you, Rube?"

McAllister knew that he must act and continued to act. He must not stop until he was clear of the situation if he was to stay alive and carry out his purpose.

He switched his knife to his left

hand, slapped the right down on the butt of the Remington, drew, cocked and fired in one movement, aiming at the sound. He heard the man cry out and go down.

Confusion broke out all around him.

A man came running through the darkness and blundered into him. He cursed and McAllister swung the Remington high, bringing the barrel down with all his strength. He missed the head and thought he caught the man on the shoulder.

"Christ!" the fellow exclaimed.

McAllister triggered and fired.

Somebody not far off started firing in his direction and a man was yelling with the strident note of alarm: "They're out here. They're among us."

McAllister turned and fled. He ran a dozen yards and dropped to the ground and listened to the effect of his silent attack in the darkness. Shouts of instruction and advice came from all directions and there was panic in every voice except one he recognized as that of Joe Church.

"Pull back. Every one of you pull back."

McAllister heard the sound of men running. One came near him and he snapped a shot at him and rapidly moved his own position as shots were sent back in return.

He lay still until the sounds died away. Most of the men who had been near the barn had pulled back through the darkness further along the bench. He reckoned he couldn't do much more damage in that direction.

He started to crawl uphill.

Taking his time and still stopping every now and then to listen, he worked his way uphill till he knew that he had passed the trench by at least a hundred feet. Then he worked his way north till he was above the trench. He was relying on the fact that the gunmen would be occupying the trench.

He lay on the soft sod of the bench, still damp from the rain, and waited.

After ten minutes, he heard the sound of men's voices and moved in on them.

Within minutes he could hear the words distinctly.

"What in hell do you think happened down there?"

"Sounded like one of them got outa the house."

"Yeah. But I reckon he didn't get far. It's quiet enough now."

To him it sounded as if there were three men in the rifle-pit. They were stationed there in good cover, waiting for the dawn when they would be able to open fire on the house from their vantage point. McAllister reckoned on cutting down on them in the first glimmer of light, but his chance came sooner than he expected.

Suddenly, not ten yards from him, there was a flare of light. One of the men thinking that he was safe from being seen from below had lighted a smoke.

McAllister moved faster than he had ever moved before.

He tore the Remington from leather, raised himself, cocked and fired.

The still night seemed to be split by the sound of the shot. The match was dropped.

A man shouted.

McAllister ran forward a half-dozen paces, halted and fired. A man's voice expressed fear and he cocked and fired again and again.

A shot came back his way. He fired at the muzzle flash and side-stepped to make himself less of a certain target. But he must have stepped into a shot, for something clipped his knee sharply and when he took another pace to the side, his leg collapsed under him and he fell to the ground. But he did not lose his gun. He lay flat and thrust the Remington out at arm's length along the ground and emptied it at the flash that came. He rolled then and started to hastily reload. Feet pounded off down the hill.

He waited; a groan came from the pit.

Dawn came slowly.

The man in the pit was groaning.

Before it became light enough for him to be seen from below McAllister wormed his way forward and carefully looked over the edge of the trench, his gun ready for trouble.

The first thing he saw was the face of a dead man with a neat bullet hole through the center of his forehead. Not a pretty sight to meet any time, still less in the cold light of dawn. McAllister's stomach heaved once and became steady.

The second man was still alive. It was he who was moaning. McAllister didn't know him, but he had hardcase written all over him.

McAllister slid down into the trench, wincing from the pain in his leg. It had stiffened up badly in the cold of the night, exposed on the bench.

The man had been hit in one shoulder, high. McAllister reckoned he'd live. Which added a complication.

McAllister said: "Who're you?"

The man opened his eyes and stared at him.

"McAllister!"

"In person."

"I'm dyin'."

McAllister laughed dryly.

"You ain't dyin'. You just ought to be. You get outa here. You're foulin' the place up an' there ain't room for the two of us."

"I can't move."

McAllister said coldly: "Boy, you move outa here inside a count of three or I plant one where your pard got his'n."

The man groaned again.

"It'd kill me to move."

"Suits me fine. Let's start the count. One."

The man sat up, clutching his shoulder.

"Two."

The man got his feet up to him and with a hand on the side of the trench, staggered to his feet. He looked awful.

He gave McAllister an appealing and despairing look, but the big man felt no pity for him. The women and children down below were on his mind.

"Git," he said and the man started to heave himself over the edge of the pit.

There was a stutter of shots from below. The man said: "Ugh!" and fell back against the far side of the trench and landed on his dead comrade. McAllister turned him over and saw that a bullet had taken him through the heart.

"Godammit," he said, "that makes two of 'em to pitch out."

He holstered his revolver and started work. It was no easy task with his injured leg and it took him the best part of half-an-hour with the men below trying to get him with their rifles, but he finally made it. He then started his own part of the war.

He had left to him in the trench three rifles, all repeaters, and six boxes of ammunition. It was a treasure trove that delighted him.

He looked at the battle.

The attackers had drawn in as close as they could to the house and three men had occupied the rifle pit over by the creek. That meant that the house was being attacked now on three sides, for he heard sounds of shooting from the rear that showed the attacking force had worked its way around during the hours of darkness. But he held the left flank and he was above the enemy. He'd play hell with them, if they had put some men up in the rocks above him. But he thought not, because they would be satisfied by the three men they had thought they had in this very pit.

He checked that the three rifles were loaded and started.

First, he started on the men behind the ruined barn and drove them out of there. They tried running back, but the men in the house spotted them and knocked one of them over. He lay out in the open kicking away his life. McAllister was pleased. The attackers had already taken more losses than such professionals like to suffer.

He now started on the men lying out there in the long grass, most of whom were nearly completely out of sight of the defenders in the house. He himself could not see many of them clearly, but he glimpsed their rifle-smoke and laid his shots down on that. Within a short time, he had them moving back out of range. That left the only real danger to the house to the rear and in the other rifle pit. This last was a long shot from him and it would take superb shooting to move them. He could see into the pit clearly, but he wished that he had his own Henry with him, for such shooting he needed a weapon he knew.

He chose a Remington repeater from the weapons he had in the pit and started. Maybe he didn't hit anybody, but he sure made the men in the pit get their heads down. But while he was at this, he received shots from his rear and swinging around, he saw that he was being attacked by men from the back of the house.

He faced them and a shooting match started. He had the advantage of good cover, but he reckoned that there were at least three of them. He fought back savagely. He was relieved to see after a few minutes shooting that somebody in the house had spotted the attack on him and at least one rifle opened up on the men from there. This new fire pushed them back. They retired into the rocks above and contented themselves with lobbing shots down onto him from there. The rocks were too far away from the house to fire on the building, but he was just within range and, although the shots did not come too close, he was uncomfortable where he was and had to keep his head down. Which ruled out his usefulness in this position.

Head down and with lead splattering around him, he considered the position. He either had to stay this way till dark or he had to get those men above out of the rocks.

He stayed where he was, for he had no choice and the fight limped on through the day. Luckily the former occupants of the trench had food and water with them, so he didn't starve. But it was cramped in the trench and his leg was troubling him. The bullet that had glanced off his knee had done no great damage, but it had burst the skin enough to make it bleed badly and was painful. With his knife, he cut his pants and tied the wound up tightly with his bandanna. That had to suffice.

He was still there crouched under the rifle-fire from above when night came. This, he knew, was the danger time. Joe Church would have become impatient. His men would want this business finished. Which meant that they would either rush the house or set fire to it or both.

As soon as it was dark, he crawled out of the trench. One, he didn't want to be jumped in the dark by the men above and two, he had another objective in mind.

14

AROUND midnight, his leg was giving him hell after so much walking, and he found their horses.

They were in a dell and there were two men with them. Two men who weren't expecting trouble. Why should they? There was something like forty men attacking a handful of nesters in a shack. Who would expect one of the defenders to be this far down the bench?

They had a fire going and they were cooking small hunks of beef in the flames on the ends of sticks. The smell of coffee reached McAllister as he crouched behind a clump of brush.

He stayed where he was for some time, just to be sure that there were no more than two men there. And while he waited, something interesting happened.

A man came walking out of the darkness from the direction of the battle which still popped in the distance. He carried a rifle and he looked pooped.

One of the men at the fire said: "Hi, Al. You hit or somethin'?"

"Naw," the man said. "I'm lightin' out."

"Joe won't be too pleased about that."

"I should worry."

"How about your pay?"

"What's the good of pay if'n you're daid? You know there's been eight men killed. Eight men dead, good men, and all we're up against is a lousy bunch of nesters."

He walked over to the picket line of horses, picked one out, saddled it and with a word of farewell, rode out into the darkness.

McAllister grinned to himself.

He rose from his hiding place and walked toward the fire. One of the men turned his head and called out: "Who's this?"

McAllister said: "Bill."

The man rose and asked: "Bill who?"

McAllister drew his gun and said: "Don't move."

They raised their hands instinctively and McAllister told them to turn around. They obeyed him. That was a point in favor of gunmen as enemies — they respected guns and knew what they could do. He relieved them of their weapons and tossed them away into the darkness.

One of them said: "It's McAllister, isn't it?"

"Right first time."

"What happens to us?"

"A good question. You walk along the bench till you find Joe Church. You tell him that I have a posse on the way from town. It'll be a big posse. I'll see to that. He won't have a chance."

One man said: "You ain't goin' to get away with this, mister."

McAllister smiled.

"You ain't goin' to be the one to stop me, that's for sure," he said. "Now, get walkin'."

Reluctantly, they walked north into the darkness. McAllister knew they might try something, but that was a risk he had to take. He would like to have seen Joe Church's face when he heard the news. He holstered his revolver and ran to the horses, throwing a hull on a nice-looking bay and bridling it. He slipped the picket-line, fired a couple of shots under the tail of the nearest horse and mounted the bay.

He stayed for a moment, listening to the sound of the horses disappearing down the bench into the night and started out himself. He had a long ride in front of him and he had to weigh speed against safety, for it was no easy matter riding in this kind of country in the dark at any speed. But he had to get help to the beleaguered house before it was too late.

He took it easy going down off the bench and until he hit the valley trail, then the clouds cleared a little and he rode by starlight, stepping up the speed till he reached a flat run. He kept the horse at it for as long as he could, then, as he came out of the valley onto the sweep of the high prairie, he brought the animal down to a swinging fox-trot for several miles before he put it to a gallop again. He reckoned this animal wouldn't be much good for anything ever again by the time he got it to town.

Dawn found him going down Main Street on a horse that was dying on its feet. He wasn't in a much better condition himself. When he halted outside Bright's store, he slid exhausted from the saddle. The horse hung its head and stood on splayed legs.

McAllister walked to the door of the store and hammered on it with his fist.

After a minute Bright appeared and opened the door.

"My God," he said at sight of

McAllister, "you look all in, man. What happened?"

"Everythin' happened," McAllister told him. "Joe Church and forty or so gunmen have a handful of nesters cornered in my house. They have women and children with them. One woman was killed."

"Come on in."

McAllister walked in on legs of rubber and sat down.

"How soon can you get a posse together?"

"I can have ten good men within the hour."

"That ain't enough men and it ain't soon enough."

"Maybe I can do better than that," the sheriff said.

McAllister snarled: "You bet your God-damned life you can do better'n that. Now, move."

Startled, the sheriff whipped off his apron and ran out onto the street. McAllister rose slowly, walked to Bright's office to the rear of the store and lay down on the floor. Within seconds he was asleep.

It seemed that he hadn't been asleep for a minute when a rough hand woke him. He stirred, opened his eyes and sat up. The office was full of men and Bright was bending over him.

"Wake up, McAllister. I have the men here and we're movin' out."

Slowly, he got to his feet and staggered stiff-legged after them as they went through the store and onto the street. It seemed that the place was full of horses and men. He counted about twenty-five men. That wasn't at all bad. They were all armed with rifles and revolvers. Some of them looked like townsmen, but that didn't matter, when they came to shooting a rifle, McAllister's experience told him they were as good as the next man.

McAllister rubbed sleep from his eyes and said: "Yeah." He went to the edge of the sidewalk and bawled for silence. They went quiet and turned their faces to him.

"Men," he said, "I reckon you're in for a bloody fight, so if any of you don't have the stomach for it, don't come. There's women an' children in my house and there's a woman been shot by the Association gunmen. Do I have to tell you anythin' more?"

An angry growl went up from the men. McAllister nodded, satisfied that these men would ride and fight.

"What're we waitin' for?" a man shouted. "Let's ride."

Somebody had switched the saddle he had ridden in on to another horse, a passable-looking sorrel. McAllister stepped wearily into the saddle. Then they were trotting down Main with the people staring at them. A small cheer went up and a rider or two waved. As they neared the edge of town, Bright, in the lead, stepped up the pace and the dust rose as the little army swept off to the south-west, heading for battle.

McAllister clamped his legs to the

side of this animal and promptly fell asleep again.

He dozed lightly, waking each time the pace of his mount changed and by mid-morning he opened his eyes wide, refreshed. They were traveling at a hammering trot down the valley and he could see the bench and the trail up to it above him. He pushed his animal forward till he was alongside the sheriff.

"Bright," he said, "they know we're comin'. Take it easy as you approach the trail."

The sheriff raised his hand and halted the posse. Bridle-chains rattled and leather creaked as men eased themselves in the saddle. They were all saddle-sore and the horses were tired. They stared up at the bench.

"I'll go forward and scout," McAllister said.

Bright nodded.

McAllister urged the sorrel forward and mounted the start of the steep trail. There was no sign of life from above. He reached halfway and nothing happened. Joe Church must be slipping. He knew that McAllister was coming, but he had not pulled men back from the house to guard the trail.

A rifle slammed flatly from above.

The sorrel squealed shrilly, stood on its hindlegs and went over backward. McAllister had time only to kick his feet free of the stirrup-irons and fling himself clear. He made a bad landing and hurt his already injured knee. He heard the horse rolling noisily down the steepness of the trail and found himself also rolling. He was brought up short by a rock and lay gasping with the wind knocked out of him. Bullets were chipping rock splinters and throwing dust up all around him.

From below he could hear Bright bellowing orders. Rifles cracked as the posse went into action.

McAllister got himself undraped from the rock and scuttled as fast as he could go into cover. His rifle was on the downed horse, so that all he had with him was his Remington revolver and his knife. So he had to get in close to be effective. He hoped to heaven that some damned fool below wouldn't put a bullet through his butt. He started climbing. He made one hell of a noise, but such was the racket going on that nobody above could hear him. He looked down and saw that the posse had all found cover. One man lay sprawled out on the trail, not moving. The horses had run off down the trail and were now placidly cropping grass.

McAllister climbed on.

He estimated that the men were right on the edge of the shelf and there were about eight of them. Either they had caught up some horses or they had had a long walk from the house. Then a dreadful thought hit McAllister. Maybe they had taken the house and had ridden back on horses from there.

He saw a head above, aimed and fired.

It was a long shot, but a man pitched

out into space, tumbled all arms and legs through the air, hit the trail and rolled. Before he had gone a yard, he was shot through by rifle bullets from below. He must have been shot to rags — which showed McAllister what kind of a fight this was going to be. No mercy would be shown by either side.

There was a momentary lull in the shooting.

From below came a shout —

"McAllister."

He turned and acknowledged the shout. He recognized Bright's voice.

"Stay where you're at. We're coming up."

A half-dozen men broke cover and started scrambling up the steep slope amid a frantic burst of rifle-fire from above. Thankfully, McAllister saw that nobody was hit. The fire from above hammered away, though, trying to stop the possemen reaching the bench.

Soon the sheriff panted and heaved up beside him. He didn't look much of the storekeeper now. There was a bloody tear along one side of his face and his nails were broken where he had clawed his way up the rocks.

"We're goin' to win this fight, McAllister," the man told him. "The boys're mad and they're after blood."

"I'm glad to hear it. Come on, let's go."

They started forward and upward together, their guns out. They were under fire all the way that forced them down onto their bellies, but they didn't stop. Nor did the men with them. They kept on coming. The fire directed at them didn't stop. Even when they reached the rim of the bench, the gunmen backed up and fired on them from the long grass from high up the sloping bench.

Common sense told McAllister that now was the time to lie low and shoot it out. But there was no time. He had to think of the people in the house. Crouching down he looked below and bellowed for the men down there to bring the horses up. And fast.

They came running, bringing the horses up into fire. Some men cowered back under the fierce hail of bullets, but Bright and McAllister set an example, by springing into the saddle and spurring off at a tangent to the right, circling the men in the grass. At once several other men followed their example and at least a half-dozen horsemen pounded across the width of the bench, low in the saddle.

Bright was slightly ahead of McAllister, turning his horse into the gunmen, shouting. He came near the first man and charged him, firing his gun. A man rose from the grass and snapped a pistol shot off. Bright reeled from the saddle and, foot caught in stirrup-iron, was dragged a few yards till the horse stopped. McAllister swept past him and rode the gunman down. With an unearthly shriek the man went down under the iron hoofs. Another man turned in the grass, shooting. Firing a difficult shot from the back of a running horse, McAllister knocked the man over and rode on to the next.

It was all over in a matter of minutes.

Four men lay dead in the long green grass, their sightless eyes staring at the clouds above them. McAllister turned his horse back to Bright and found the sheriff on his feet, clutching his left shoulder, his face working in pain and shock.

"Sit down," McAllister said. "Who knows about wounds?"

"McGettrick. He oughta. He's a doctor."

McAllister bellowed for the man. Several riders had come up from the head of the trail and one of them was the doctor. He got to work right away on the sheriff. McAllister took charge. He detailed five men to stay here and guard the head of the trail and to look after the wounded of whom there were three and to guard the prisoners of whom there were two. The sheriff produced handcuffs for the prisoners and these were clamped home. That left McAllister with sixteen men. He waited for the doctor to finish with the wounded, but he reckoned he would be needed at the house. He checked that every man had a good supply of ammunition and then they rode.

They rode hard, as if the devil himself were after them, because every man there knew that Joe Church and his men would be desperate and would want to finish this quickly. Either that or to ride out and get away scot free. This no man there intended them to do.

McAllister took the lead. He used the iron mercilessly, thinking of the women and kids up there.

15

JOE CHURCH had reached the end of the line when somebody in the house opened a shutter and waved a white flag. His men were ready to pull out, for the news that McAllister might be on his way with a posse that would take them in the rear had brought near-panic to even some of the hardest men there. Church himself believed that this was bluff, because if McAllister had had a posse at his disposal he would have had it up here for the start of the fight.

So the white flag brought Church some hope.

He was behind the ruined barn. From there he bawled for the man to come out if he wanted to talk. Lief Olsen came onto the stoop, holding the white rag in one hand and carrying no gun. Church stepped out from cover. He stood there a moment and then walked into the middle of the yard. Olsen walked towards him. When he halted he said: "We have a dead woman and dead man inside. We want to bury them."

The mention of a dead woman shook Church. He turned pale and then pulled himself together.

"All right," he said. "I'll let you bury them. Four men can come out without guns and dig a grave over by the corral there."

Olsen hesitated.

"You won't try nothin'?"

"You have my word."

Olsen looked him in the eye for a moment and said: "All right." He nodded his head and turned away.

"Wait."

The nester turned again. "Yeah?"

"We ain't waitin' around all day. You have one hour to get them both planted, then we start shootin'."

Olsen nodded again and plodded toward the house. A few minutes later

240

he and his brother came out following Jeff Wellman carrying the body of his wife. Then the massive form of Morgan Wellman appeared carrying the body of his cousin Lee.

Church thought: *Two dead from the same family and one of those a woman. These men ain't never goin' to give in. They'll all have to be killed. Might as well be one way as another.*

The little funeral procession came to a halt by the corral fence and the two dead bodies were laid on the ground. The four defenders stooped for a moment, looking around at their attackers with somber eyes and then each took a shovel that the Olsens had carried and started diggin.

From cover, Church levered a round into the breech of his rifle and pointed it at the group. The two men with him followed his example.

Church called: "Stop diggin'." They straightened themselves and turned to stare at him. "You ain't diggin' no grave. Walk over here."

Lief Olsen said evenly and without a trace of emotion in his voice: "You sneakin' bastard."

"Do like I say or you're all dead men." He raised his voice: "You in the house there. You come on out without your guns or these men get themselves killed dead."

There was a prolonged silence as the truth of the treachery came home to those who listened.

Jeff Wellman raised his voice.

"You stay put in there. I don't give a damn if'n they do kill me."

"How do you feel about that, Olsen?" Church demanded.

Lief looked this way and that.

"I can't believe I'm a-hearin' right," he said. "I can't believe even a polecat like you could do a thing like this, Church."

"Keep your mouth shut," Church said through his teeth. He shouted to the house again. "Are you comin' out or do we start shootin'. Lief Olsen gets it first."

Lief's face went mottled with helpless rage.

"Stay put," he yelled. "Leave 'em Goddam well shoot."

Church raised his rifle and fired.

Lief Olsen staggered back against the corral fence, clutched at it, lost his grasp and fell to the ground. He grasped his leg, white to the mouth with shock.

Church shouted: "The next one's through his head."

Again there was silence.

Then somebody in the house called: "We're comin' out."

Jeff Wellman yelled: "For God's sake, stay put. You can't trust this man. He'll kill us all."

Church sweated and waited.

Suddenly Morgan Wellman lifted his head and said: "Listen! Hear that?"

They all went still and listened.

Every man there heard the distant and faint crackle and pop of rifle-fire.

Eric Olsen laughed hugely and roared: "Hear that?"

Church looked at the man next to him.

"Jesus God," the man said, "That's McAllister and the posse." He started away.

"Stay still," Church roared.

"We don't have horses nor nothin'."

"There's horses in the corral. Jeb, Billy, Dyson, get those horses out here."

The men started for the corral.

Church shouted: "We still have these men of yours covered. Make a move and they're dead."

Gunmen came running from cover, clambering into the corral and catching up horses, getting onto them bareback and riding them out into the yard. Church and the two men behind the barn came out and men gave them horses. There were more than enough to go around, even though some men were mounted on wagon horses.

A man yelled: "How in hell do we get outa here? McAllister'll be comin' along the bench. Them few men won't hold them at the trail."

"They'll hold them long enough for us to reach them," Church said.

"We'll ride out over the saddle to the north," a man shouted.

"No," Church roared. "We're goin' back."

A man bawled almost in his face: "We got enough dead already, Joe. I didn't come in on this to die. Let's ride."

Church saw that there was no holding them.

It meant leaving the men at the trail-head at the mercy of the posse. What odds? he asked himself. Already he had broken his code. Would once more matter? He turned his horse and rode after the men as they streamed across the yard and went around the house.

Jeff Wellman was shrieking at the people in the house: "Get 'em. Kill the bastards."

A gun fired in the house and a man by Church pitched from the saddle.

Several of the mounted men fired back, but before they could get clear another man pitched to the ground and lay kicking there.

Jeff Wellman sprang into action. He ran to one of the downed men and yanked him, bodily to his feet. The man yelled in fear as the big man smashed him to the ground with his bare fist.

Then silence fell over the place again.

Slowly the men, woman and children came out of the house, unable to believe that it was over. The men, guns in their hands, went looking for the wounded men of the attacking force and found them laid out in the grass about a quarter of a mile along the bench. Mary Wellman ran to care for the wounded Olsen.

16

THE rain which had started to fall as the posse rode in had stopped, but the sky was sullen overhead. Black clouds no longer scudded before the wind, but a great sweep of angry vapor hung menacingly and dark over the high land. The great uplands seemed to shudder in heavy fury at the smoldering skies above.

The posse stood around in the yard while the horses heaved and blew, their heads dropped, their lines in the dust that had turned to a light mud.

McAllister ate standing up, talking with the men near him. The wounded Olsen lay on the stoop, cursing, cursing softly to himself and the world in general, because he wanted to mount and ride after the men that had done this thing to him. Mary Wellman did what she could to cook a meal at

McAllister's stove. She sent endless coffee out to them.

McAllister knew only one thing: he wanted Joe Church. He wanted him like he had never wanted anything else in this world. He was going to put the manacles on him and he was going to take him personally into trial.

After he had eaten, he walked apart from the men, thinking, trying to see clearly what he should do, how best he could come up with Church. Clearly the man had ridden from the bench over the saddle and headed north for the moment. But only for the moment. Church was a hired gun and he wouldn't clear out of the country without his pay. He would head for the Association headquarters, wherever that was. Or he would head for Rigden's place. Which?

Men must go after him, follow his trail to make sure of him, but the man who would catch him would be the one who cut him off as he went for his blood money.

Who then should McAllister deputize to go after the gunman over the saddle: Jeff Wellman was the likeliest candidate, but the man was hating too much right now. His posse would turn into a lynching party and McAllister didn't want that. This was going to be done legally. Church was going to be brought down by the nester law that he despised so much.

McAllister turned and looked the men over.

His eye fell on Murchinson, the banker, from town, a man who had said little, but who had ridden and fought well all along. He was steady and intelligent and, in spite of being a desk man, was a good horseman and knew the country well from hunting trips.

McAllister approached the man and put the proposition to him. Without fuss, the man accepted and was duly sworn in. He and McAllister then picked their men. The banker chose ten. McAllister picked Pete, Ruiz and a man named Holtz whom he had worked with in the past and knew. The rest were to return to town as fast as they could in case any of the gunmen should turn up there. If they did, they were to be arrested, lodged in jail and kept for McAllister's return. Two men were detailed to take a wagon with the wounded men, both from the house and down the bench, and take them into town.

The posse rode off north on tired horses with not much hope of catching the gunmen on their fresh mounts. Olsen and the Wellmans hitched two horses to the wagon, while McAllister and his three men tightened cinches on their tired animals and went off at a trot down the bench.

They found the sheriff sitting up and swearing. It was an education to hear him. He introduced McAllister to some new words when he was told that Church and his men had gotten away.

McAllister said: "I want to know one

thing. If Church and his men want to get paid before they pull out of the country, where would they head?"

"Rigden's."

"Don't the Association have a headquarters?"

"Rigden is the Association."

"Will Church have the nerve to ask Rigden for his money after gettin' beaten?"

"Joe Church has the nerve for anything, as well you know."

McAllister said: "That settles it," and walked to his horse. He and the three others rode down from the bench.

It was a nightmare ride. There was no great hurry, for, if Church was headed for Rigden's, it would take him some hours to get there. And McAllister couldn't have hurried if he wanted to, the horses were so tired.

The men dozed in the saddle as they rode, for there was not one of them who wasn't weary to the bone. Night overtook them halfway to

Rigden's place, but they didn't stop. They pushed on steadily through the darkness.

Dawn found them still in the saddle, heading east, the hoofs of the horses going *swish-swish* through the grass. There was no sound but this and the pounding of the horses' hoofs and the creak of leather. They rode wordlessly, knowing what lay ahead of them and they wondered each of them who would be dead by the time it was all over.

McAllister wondered too about Rose. She would be at Rigden's place and he didn't like the idea of her being mixed up in this business. There would be Rigden's wife there too.

He thought about Rigden and how he could bring a conviction against him, knowing that the man would probably be smart enough to sidestep a charge, claiming that it was the Association that had hired the gunmen and that he had nothing to do with it. Every big rancher in the country would be a worried man tonight when he heard of the defeat of Joe Church and his men. But they would think themselves bigger than the law. So somebody had to talk for McAllister's case to stand up in court. But who? Joe Church would never talk. It was against the man's code. The smaller fry would not know what had been going on. All they would know was that they had been hired. He thought about that, riding in a haze of tiredness in the cold light of dawn. They had stayed at Rigden's place. The remaining men had or would be paid by Rigden. If McAllister could prove that, he would be getting somewhere.

But there would be a fight, one hell of a fight. He felt guilty at bringing these men with him. The fight was not theirs. Pete and Ruiz were only hired men and it seemed ludicrous for them to die for wages because of their loyalty to a brand. That was the code of the west, but it didn't make sense to him right now. He had a liking for both men. Surely they had done enough.

And at the end of this, when the last shot was fired — there was Rose.

The horses pounded on and his thoughts kept time with the hammering hoofs.

Ten men rode into Rigden's yard.

Ten tired men and all that was left of the forty that had ridden out with such confidence. The rest had run out of the country, their lives more important than their pay, or they lay back there wounded on the bench, or they were dead. The ten men were bitter, disillusioned and so tired that they scarcely knew what they were doing. The horses stood with hanging heads and splayed legs. The men dismounted stiffly, watching the house, waiting for Rigden to appear. They looked at Joe Church, waiting for his lead. Church stood as dead-faced as the rest of them.

They were all mildly surprised when Burt Rigden stepped out from among them and said: "I'll go fetch my father." He had been silent till now so that they had forgotten that the son of the man who paid them had been riding with them all the while.

They watched him, dead-eyed, as he walked from the horses to the house, his spurs making light music as he walked.

As he went, he thought: *The old man's up at the window there. He watched us come in. He knows already.* And it was strange. For the first time in his life he wasn't afraid of facing his father. After the experience of the last few days, he wasn't afraid of anything on earth. He had come through what he thought was a living hell and he would never be the same again.

His powerful legs were tired now and his strong body seemed to groan at every step he took. But there was something fresh and clean inside him and he was inspired by its presence. He was a simple man and he didn't examine himself, but he knew that he was as he had never been before.

As he stepped into the house, his father was coming down the stairs. Burt halted inside the door and waited till his father reached the last step.

"Well?" Rigden demanded, his voice a bass rumble.

"We were beaten," he said.

Rigden's mouth became ugly. The vein on his forehead swelled dark against his mottled face.

"What?"

"They beat us. You didn't hire enough gunmen."

Rigden came two paces forward, his rage terrible to see.

"You yellow-bellied whelp. You stand there . . ." The words choked in his throat. He was beside himself.

Burt thought: *I ain't afraid of you, you old bastard*.

He said: "Watch your words, pa. I'm liable to ram 'em down your throat."

Brett came out of a side door and stood gaping there. He was still pale from his wound.

For a moment, Rigden looked as if he had been struck. He looked hard at his son as though he could not believe his ears and, then, with a bellow of fury, he hurled himself at Burt and smashed him to the ground with his fists. Rigden stood over the boy for a moment, breathing hard, before he turned and stamped out of the house.

Brett looked down at Burt and laughed nervously.

"You asked for it," he said.

Burt got to his feet and wiped the blood from the corner of his mouth with the back of his hand.

"That's the last time he strikes me," he said hoarsely. "An' take that smirk off'n your fool face or I'll knock it off." He walked out of the house and stood on the stoop looking at his father's back, his hand on his gun, knowing the terrible truth that he was near killing his own father.

Rigden was saying to the men in the yard —

"What you come back here for, huh?

Why you come ridin' back in here? You win a fight or somethin'? You proud of yourselves? The great heroes. My God, the sight of you-all sickens me to my belly."

Joe Church stepped forward and stood looking up at the man on the stoop.

"We come for our pay, Mr. Rigden."

"You what?" There was utter disbelief in Rigden's voice.

"We come for our pay."

"You'll get no pay from me. I hired you to clean out a ragged bunch of nesters. You mean you think you earned money ridin' around the country shootin' off your guns? You mean I should pay you for *that*? You think I'm green or somethin'?" The man actually stamped his feet in a paroxysm of fury. He looked like a mottle-faced frantic puppet. A deadly dancing doll.

"You'll get no pay from me, Church. That's final. You-all get on those crowbaits of yours and ride out."

"We'll do that fast enough when we get our pay."

Rigden jumped down from the stoop.

"Take your asses outa here," he shouted. "You'll not get a dime."

There was a brief moment of silence.

Church's right hand moved and there was a gun in it. They all heard it come to full cock. It was pointed at Rigden's belly. The man went very still.

"We'll take our pay any way you want," Church said. His voice was cold and he stood very straight.

The gunmen moved instinctively. Each man drew his gun and those nearest the bunkhouse turned and faced it. The cowhands who had come outside stared down the barrels of the guns.

Rigden said through his teeth: "You'll hang for this."

"No more talk," Church said. "The money."

Rigden stared at him for a moment, looking as though his hand itched to touch his gun at his side. But if he had any idea of resistance, he thought better of it. Turning, he mounted the stoop and walked along it to his office. Church followed him, not taking his gun from his back. They went into the office. Rigden took keys from his pocket and went down on one knee before the safe in the corner of the room.

As he knelt there, he looked into the grim face of ruin. He was certain that these men would not just take their pay. They would clean him out. They were gunmen. He had borrowed heavily to finance the cleaning out of the nesters and if they took everything that was in the safe, he would be finished. He was surprised when he heard Church say: "We'll take eleven thousand dollars. That's what's owing to us."

It was the exact amount of money that he would owe this number of men, yet if he paid it without his scheme coming to fruition, it would still mean ruin for him. He agonized as he opened the safe and swung open its heavy door.

He took the money out, straightened and went to his desk with it.

"You'll be outside the law after this, Church," he said. "You know that."

"We were all outside the law when you hired us," Church said coolly. "We all know that."

Rigden counted the money with trembling fingers. When he finished, he said: "That's it. Pick it up and get outa here."

A sound at the door made them both turn. The man called Gafferty walked in at the door. He stopped and looked at the money on the table. He was not one of Church's hired gunmen, but he had fought with them all through the little war. He worked for a Scottish financed outfit to the north-west. He held a gun in his hand.

He said: "We'll take the pay for all the men you hired, Rigden," he said.

Rigden said: "You get outa here, Gafferty. I didn't hire you."

"But I earned your pay. There's some of the boys in town waiting for their money. I'll take it to them, plus a small bonus for myself."

Rigden shouted: "You damn fool. You'll never work in this country again if'n you do this."

"If I do this I'll never want to work again. Empty that safe, Rigden."

The rancher turned to Church.

"You ain't goin' to stand for this, Church?" he demanded.

Church said: "All I care about is my money." He reached forward and took the money in his left hand from the desk. "Thanks. I'll be goin'."

Two men stepped into the opening of the doorway. They both held guns in their hands. One of them said: "I like what you said, Gafferty."

Church stepped forward.

"I have our pay here, boys," he said.

"I'm takin' a bonus," the man said.

"Me too," the other added.

Rigden pleaded with Church.

"For God's sake, Church," he said, "you ain't goin' to let 'em get away with this."

Church walked to the door and turned.

"I have my pay," he said. "That's all I care about. If you want me I shall be in town for a few days. Tell McAllister that if he comes this way, he'll want to see me an' I'll be waitin' for him."

He walked out.

The other riders watched him as he went to his horse and stuffed the money in his saddlebags.

"We'll split it over the next ridge, boys," he said. "There's trouble here. Let's go." He stepped quickly into the saddle and turned his horse. Some of the men followed him as he went out of the yard, but two or three stayed still, watching the door to Rigden's office.

Their horses jumped a little when a sound of a shot came from the office. Two men at once came hurrying out. Both men had money bags in their left hands and one held a smoking revolver.

They leapt down the stoop steps and ran for their horses.

Hardy Rigden came staggering to the office door and stood there for a moment. He held a gun in his hand and he shouted incoherently.

Pandemonium broke loose.

Burt Rigden standing at the house door, drew his gun and fired after Gafferty and missed him. Rigden fired and Brett Rigden, running from the house with a gun in his hand, also fired at the little group of horsemen. The men whom Church was leading away at once put spurs to their animals and went out of there fast.

One of the horsemen pitched from the saddle and the animal reared in panic.

Willy Toff and Strange, outside the bunkhouse, ran back inside, either to hide or to get their guns. One of the horsemen drew and fired. A window of the house crashed inward with a tinkle of glass. Another horseman fired several rapid shots and turned his horse to escape from the flying lead. Hardy Rigden fell forward over the stoop rail and dropped his gun into the yard.

Rigden fell onto the boards of the stoop yelling: "Kill the bastards. They've gotten all my money. Kill 'em." He ended in a frantic scream.

Brett ran down the yard, yelling and firing hysterically as he went. Gafferty turned in the saddle and calmly gunned him down. The boy fell into the dust and his shouting turned to the whimper of a hurt animal. Burt fired several times at Gafferty but missed for the man was on the move now, lying along his horse's neck and using the spurs ferociously. The rest of the horsemen took off after him.

As they disappeared from the yard, two women ran out of the house, Rigden's wife and Rose. Margaret ran to Rigden, crying over him, Rose stood on the stoop looking bemused. Burt walked down to Brett and turned him over with his toe so that he lay on his back. When Toff and Strange came out of the bunkhouse with guns in their hands, he said to them: "Carry him into the house. He's been hit in the belly; go easy with him."

They put their guns away and lifted the inert form of the boy. As they went into the house, Rose turned and followed them. Burt turned to his father, gently pulled his mother away from the fallen man.

He looked down at his father and saw that his face had gone gray. The man was badly in shock and his hands trembled violently. His eyes were open and he stared fixedly at his elder son.

Burt looked for the wound and found it deep in the left shoulder.

He holstered his gun and started to get the man to his feet, Rigden knocked his hand aside and muttered: "I don't need none of your damned help." Slowly, very slowly, he heaved himself to his feet and stood leaning against the stoop upright. He looked at his wife.

"They cleaned me out," he said

hoarsely. "I'm finished."

"Let's get you inside and I'll clean that wound," his wife said.

Tiredly, he walked into the house. At every step they thought that he would fall, but his willpower took him along. He went to Brett lying on a couch in the parlor. He was bleeding badly and already the couch seemed soaked with blood. Willy Toff and Strange stood by looking helpless.

Rigden said: "Willy, take the fastest horse you can find and ride to town for the doctor. If he won't come, put your gun on him."

"Willy said: "Yes, sir, Mr. Rigden," and hurried out of the house.

"Strange, you get outa here."

The man walked out.

Margaret was on her knees beside her son, weeping. Rose stood in the background, her face ashen. Rigden pushed his wife roughly aside and said: "There ain't time for that foolishness. Git me whiskey, hot water and carbolic. I'll fix the boy till the doc comes."

Both women hurried away to do his bidding.

Rigden demanded Burt's help. Together they leaned Brett against the back of the couch and drew up his knees so that there would be a chance of the abdominal wound being closed.

"If there's lead in there," Rigden said, "it has to come out."

"Wait for the doc," Burt said.

"But we have to stop the bleeding."

The women came in with the whiskey, hot water and carbolic. He poured carbolic into the bowl and took a large swig of whiskey from the bottle. That brought some color back into his cheeks and some life into his dead eyes. His face was twisted from the pain of his own wound. He got down on his knees beside his younger son and opened his clothes to look at the wound. Blood was still oozing from it. He paused for a moment, unnerved by the sight, but pulled himself together and started work.

17

IN sight of the house, McAllister halted.

Everything there semed unnaturally quiet and still.

"Pete," he said. "Get over by the corner of the corral and cover the yard. Ruiz, watch the bunkhouse. Holtz, I reckon you'd best side me."

They nodded. McAllister and Holtz kneed their horses forward and headed for the house. As they crossed the yard, a man came out of the bunkhouse and stared at them without making a move against them. It was Strange.

As they neared the house, the door opened and Burt Rigden stepped out. Rose came out after him. She and McAllister looked at each other and McAllister thought that she looked even more beautiful than before. He gave her a little smile and she gave him a wavering one back.

To Burt, he said: "I'm looking for Joe Church. Has he been here?"

"He was here," Burt said. McAllister noticed that the boy's voice was curiously dead. "But he went."

Rose said quickly: "There's been shooting. The men came here. I don't know what happened, but the men were shooting."

McAllister stepped down from the saddle.

"What happened, Burt?" he asked.

"Joe Church came in, spoke with my father and rode out with some of the men," the boy said. "Then some of the men put their guns on my father and robbed him. They emptied the safe. Come inside. My father wanted to see you."

"Wants to see me?" McAllister was surprised.

"Yes. Come on into the house."

McAllister turned to Holtz —

"Come on in, Henry," he said. "I want a witness to this." Holtz dismounted and the four of them walked into the house. Burt led them into the parlor and there they found Rigden and Brett lying on the couch. McAllister saw the bandage around Rigden's shoulder. The upper part of his body was naked, but he draped a coat over his shoulders.

Rigden didn't waste time.

"You ain't the sheriff," he said. "But I reckon you'll do, McAllister. I have a complaint to swear out." McAllister nodded. He had to admire the cool nerve of the man.

"Who against?"

"Man named Gafferty."

"One of your imported gunmen?"

Rigden flushed.

"He rides for the Highland Cattle Company. He robbed me. He shot me an' he shot my son. If the boy dies, Gafferty'll hang."

McAllister walked over and looked down at the unconscious boy. The face was as pale as death, the eyes still and closed. He turned to the father.

"Where'd he get it?"

"In the belly. Doc says it's a fifty-fifty chance."

"And you want the law to take a hand?"

"That's what you're paid for."

McAllister saw that Mrs. Rigden had come into the room. Rose put an arm around her shoulders.

"You import an army of gunmen, you burn a half-dozen homes," McAllister said in a steady voice, "you kill several good men and a woman. And now you want the law to kill your snakes for you."

Some of the fire that had been missing from Rigden's manner showed itself again.

"Don't you come a-walkin' in here, gettin' lippy, mister," he said. "You git on your hoss and tote yourself into town an' do what you're paid for."

Henry Holtz said: "Rem, I'm itchin' to bend my gun barr'l over this coyote's haid." Rigden gave him an outraged look, as if to demand how dare a common rider speak that way about a Rigden.

"I know you, man, an' I ain't likely to forget you," he said.

McAllister said: "Mrs. Rigden, it might be best if you left the room. What I have to do isn't pleasant."

Rigden barked: "What's this?"

"Rigden, ask your wife to leave the room."

"I don't carry out the wishes of a man like you for the askin'. She stays."

Heavily, McAllister said: "All right, she stays. Let her stay and see the final humiliation."

"What in hell're you talkin' about?"

"I'm arrestin' you."

There was a short silence in the room that was broken by Rigden demanding: "An' what're you chargin' me with?"

"I won't know what the fancy words are till I get a lawyer to dress 'em up, but I reckon there's witnesses that say you imported hired gunmen to burn out the nesters."

Mrs. Rigden said: "Hardy, is this true?"

To his wife he snarled shortly: "Hold your tongue, woman." He swung on McAllister. "You can't prove a thing. Those men were brought in by the Cattle Association. My God, the Association has the approval of the governor. This time you've bitten off more'n you can chew, McAllister."

"The governor ain't above the law like you think you are, Rigden. An' I have witnesses like I said. The men bunked here, fed here and, I reckon, was paid here."

"You can arrest the hired men as fast as you like," Rigden said, "but you can't touch me."

"I'm touching you."

McAllister looked at the women and continued: "I don't want to make a show of arms in front of the ladies."

Rigden laughed.

"I don't have no such compunction," he said and drew his gun. Burt who stood near the door drew his.

Holtz looked like a man trapped, but McAllister didn't seem ruffled.

"You always act in character," McAllister said. "I knew this would be your attitude. I left two men outside and they have their rifles trained on the house. You'll gain nothin' by holin' me here. But I'll tell you what I'll do. What I intended to do when I saw that boy lying shot half to death there. I'll ride now and I'll catch up with the man that did it. He'll hang. An' I'll be back for you, Rigden. You can stay with your boy till the doc's sure whether he'll live or die."

Rose said: "Hardy, put up your gun and you too, Burt. This isn't the time for guns. There've been enough men shot."

Rigden growled: "There'll be more shot before I'm finished." He gave a short coughing laugh. "All right," he said, "you go after Church and Gafferty. By God, they'll settle your hash for you. The next time I see you will be in a pine coffin."

He put away his gun and made a sign to Burt to do the same with his.

McAllister walked to the door and turned.

"If I don't come out," he said, "let me have news of Brett in town." Then he walked out into the yard. Rose went to follow him, but Rigden caught her by the arm and held her back.

"None of my women is runnin' after that kind," he said.

She looked down coldly at the hand that held her.

"Let go of me," she said. "I'm not one of your women and never was."

Slowly, he released her and she walked out into the yard.

McAllister and Holtz were in the saddle. She walked up to the big man and laid a hand on his knee.

"Be careful," she said, "for my sake."

He looked down at her and smiled.

"I'm always careful, honey," he said. "But I'll be extra careful. I've got good reason now."

Burt had come out onto the stoop

and was watching them.

McAllister bent and touched her cheek with his rope-gnarled hand, then turned his horse and trotted the tired animal out of the yard. Holtz followed him. Pete and Ruiz ran to their animals and vaulted into the saddle. At the ridge, McAllister turned in the saddle and lifted a hand to her in salute. Slowly, she walked back into the house.

Burt gave her a somber smile as she passed him and said: "It's like that is it, Rose?"

She smiled back at him and said: "Yes," and went on into the house.

18

IT was night when they came into town on horses that were even more bushed than the men. McAllister led the way to the livery stable, through streets that showed only the occasional pedestrian and very little hoofed traffic.

A lamp was burning in the livery yard and an old man, limping on a stove-in leg, came out to greet them.

"Howdy, gents," he said, then he caught sight of Pete's Indian face and Ruiz's Mexican one and looked as if he hadn't used the word 'gents'.

McAllister got down stiffly.

"Water and feed the horses," he said. "Give them a good rub down. Three of us will sleep in your hay."

The old man gobbled like a turkey cock.

"I'll keer for the hosses," he said,

"but you ain't sleepin' in no hay. Again orders."

McAllister lifted the badge on his vest.

"That says we do," he said.

"My orders says you don't."

McAllister smiled and lifted his gun from its holster.

"This says we do too," he said, "and it says you don't go into town blabberin' we're here."

The old man swallowed his adam's apple a couple of times and nodded. Without a word he picked up the horses' lines and led the animals away.

McAllister turned to Holtz.

"We can't all sleep yet, Henry," he said. "You know the town and the folks in it. Go have some drinks in the saloon and keep your ears and eyes open. I want Church and Gafferty and any of the other men who rode with them. But mostly I want Church and Gafferty. If you find out for sure, come back here and get some shut-eye. Any road, don't wake us till a half-hour before dawn. All right?"

"All right," Holtz said and walked to the gate on legs of rubber

"Hit the hay," McAllister told the other two and the three of them walked into the barn. The lamps at the door lit the interior dimly. McAllister placed his men and himself strategically. Pete up in the loft, Ruiz to the left down the further end of the barn alongside the half-dozen horses that stood there in stalls. He himself went deep into the building back and slightly to the right of the door just beyond the faint circle of light from the lamp. "And keep your boots on and your hands on your gun-butts," he told the other two.

They went to their positions, lay down in the hay and within seconds were all asleep. McAllister's last thought was of Rose and whether he would live to enjoy life with her.

With all the somberness of his last waking thought, he slept deeply till a hand rested lightly on his arm. He sat up with hay in his hair and his gun in his hand.

It was Holtz.

"I found Gafferty," he said. "He's pulling out now. He's down at the Gimpson Corral with a half-dozen others saddling up."

McAllister reached for his hat and slapped it on his head. Picking hay out of his clothes, he asked: "What about Church?"

"He'll wait for you. He expects you to come after him."

So it was going to be a stand up fight between the two of them. The thought sent a cold chill of apprehension through him, but it suited him. It was the only way this thing between him and Church could ever end. One of them had to die.

He went and woke Pete and Ruiz. They came grumbling from their sleep, stamping out into the lamplight and blinking. McAllister told them what Holtz had already told him.

"So what do we do, patron?" Ruiz asked.

"We go take him."

"They out-number us."

"I know that."

They checked their guns by the light of the lamp and the old man appeared in the doorway, chewing on his gums.

"There goin' to be trouble, deputy?"

"Only for the other fellers," McAllister told him and they walked across the yard to the gate. The nerves of each man became taut. They knew that the men ahead of them would not be taken easily. McAllister's conscience hurt him a little at bringing Pete and Ruiz into this, but he needed them along. He doubted if he could have gotten rid of them if he had wanted.

McAllister turned right at the gate of the livery and started down Main. His injured leg was sore and stiff after the hours in the saddle and the short sleep in the hay. He would have liked a stiff drink, but there wasn't time now. He worked his right hand and shifted the gun holster a little as it lay high on his right hip. He was nervous and he knew it. He was still tired and his reactions were slow.

Halfway down Main they reached the intersection with Fremont and turned right again. They walked abreast with arms' lengths between them.

They came in sight of the corral and knew it by the sight of the lights showing there. They slowed their pace instinctively and finally stopped.

McAllister said: "Fan out. Ruiz, get over the other side of the corral and don't shoot till I do. Not unless you have to. Pete, up against the buildings, there yonder. Keep your fool head down. Henry, put some more space between us, but side me. Any man gets hit, he gets a month's pay docked."

Ruiz spat into the dust and moved off.

Pete started to croon a little medicine song to himself. He eased himself to the right and got close to the buildings. There wasn't much cover for him there.

McAllister and Holtz moved on ahead. McAllister wished that he had a shotgun with him. Something devastating was needed here.

Dawn came slowly as they advanced. The lights from the lamps grew pale. They could see the men in the corral like wraiths, tightening cinches, testing ropes on the pack-animals. The place semed full of men and animals, now and then a man's voice reached them.

The corral was surrounded by a low adobe wall. When McAllister reached it, he found that it came up to his chest. He looked for Gafferty but couldn't find him. He looked to the left and saw that Holtz was in place against the wall, his gun in his hand. McAllister reached the Remington from leather and cocked it.

"Gafferty," he shouted.

The men in the corral went still. Heads turned.

"Who's this?" a man called.

"McAllister."

It happened quickly. A gun went off

and a bullet hit the top of the wall near McAllister's face, throwing adobe dust into his eyes. Holtz fired back as McAllister recoiled. Men dove all over the place for cover, they shouted, guns went off. Ruiz fired from the other side of the corral and Pete ran in from the street, leaned over the wall and started shooting.

McAllister roared: "Hold your fire. Hold your fire."

Strangely, the shooting stopped all at once, gunsmoke drifted acrid on the chill morning air.

"I want Gafferty," McAllister bellowed. "Come on out, man. No call for men to get killed over this."

A man shouted back: "You're the only one goin' to get killed, McAllister." A shot followed. McAllister saw the smoke and sent a shot at it. A man stepped out from behind a shed on stiff legs, walked two paces and crumpled to the ground.

To the right of the corral beyond this shed behind which the shot man had been hiding was a long open-fronted shed which ran almost half the length of the corral. It was in poor repair and seemed to house a collection of articles that always seem to gather in such places. There was a plough, a wagon that had seen better days, a buggy with a wheel missing, a pile of hay and a wheel-barrow, a large packing case or two and behind these articles most of the men had taken cover.

McAllister called to Holtz: "Pin 'em down there, Henry. I'm goin' around."

He set off to the right, running doubled up till he was out of sight of the men inside the corral and he found himself in front of the house that stood there. He straightened up as he passed Pete and went into the yard of this house. As he ran around the house, he came face to face with an ashen-featured man.

"My God," the man exclaimed, "what's goin' on?"

McAllister went by him without a word and ran on till he came to the rear of the open shed. The rear of the shed was the corral wall. On McAllister's side of the wall was another and smaller shed in the yard of the house. McAllister holstered his gun, heaved himself onto the roof of this smaller shed and looked down at the larger one. The roof was flat and rotten. From where he was he could see Pete, Holtz and Ruiz. He didn't doubt that they could see him and would hold their fire when he made his move. He knew that he was crazy to do it, but that was the way things went with him. He didn't think when once he got the bit between his teeth. He saw what he thought was the only thing to do and he did it. As his old man had said on more than one occasion: It didn't matter how crazy a thing was so long as it was totally unexpected. He almost laughed to himself. The men underneath him wouldn't expect this.

He drew his gun and took a deep breath.

He leapt into the air and launched

himself forward, landing with both feet on the rotten roof of the long shed. There was a rending crash, it held for no longer than a second and then he plummeted through and down.

Going through hurt his injured knee, but his pain was nothing to that of the man on whom he handed. His heels caught the fellow on the head and the two of them stretched their length on the ground. It was a shock to both of them, but the other's shock was the greater. McAllister rolled clear of him and came up shooting at the first thing that moved. This was a man standing about ten feet from him. The heavy bullet caught him in the side and smashed him against the wagon behind which he had found cover.

The old gun-fighting habit was on McAllister now. Crouched down, his right wrist locked like iron, he pivoted, cocked and fired.

A man was turning at the other end of the shed, gun up and mouth open, startled by McAllister's unexpected entry. Without conscious thought, McAllister fired. The man fell backward, clutching at himself, gun falling to the ground.

McAllister threw himself down now as two unseen guns opened up on him. But now the men on the other side of the corral were pouring lead into the end of the shed away from McAllister. He heard it striking the buggy and slamming into the adobe wall. Men cried out and one ran insanely out into the corral in an effort to catch one of the horses that were now careering wildly around the place. He managed to catch one and turned it frantically toward the gate, but a bullet plucked him from the saddle as if he were no heavier than a rag-doll and dumped him on the ground.

There was a sudden lull in the deafening roar of guns.

McAllister shouted: "Walk out into the corral with your hands up."

Two guns came flying out of the shed and landed in the dust. Then two men walked slowly out into the corral. One of them was Gafferty. Both looked like men deeply in shock.

McAllister picked himself up and walked into the open.

Holtz came through the gate. Pete and Ruiz came over the wall. Henry Holtz was clutching his right shoulder and Ruiz had a bullet-graze along one side of his face. They all looked like men who had been somewhere they wouldn't want to go again.

McAllister asked: "You all right, Henry?"

Holtz nodded stolidly.

"I'm all right."

A man ran into the open gateway and stared at them.

McAllister told him: "Go fetch a doctor, fast." He turned and looked at Gafferty and said: "Where's the money?"

"In the saddlebags on the strawberry roan."

Ruiz caught the horse and took the saddlebags from behind the saddle, handing them to McAllister who slung them over his left shoulder.

McAllister said: "Tie these two together. Tight."

He put his gun away after he had reloaded it and walked into the shed to look at the wounded. The man he had knocked out when he came through the roof was stirring. McAllister took him by the scruff of the neck and took him to the others to tie up. Then he went and looked at the wounded men.

The fellow by the wagon had received a bullet in the left shoulder. He sat with his shoulders against the wheel, looking pretty sick and sorry for himself.

"You'll live," McAllister told him not unkindly. "Doctor'll be here soon."

He walked over to the man at the other end of the shed and found that he had received a glancing bullet high in the chest near the throat. It had bounced off the top of the breastbone. It would hurt like hell for a long time, but there was no real damage done. Next, McAllister walked into the corral again and looked at the man the boys had shot off his horse. He was dead.

He reckoned the battle hadn't lasted five minutes.

He stood and looked around him, feeling tired to the bone. A man ran into the corral saying that he was the owner and wanted to know in no uncertain terms who was going to pay for the shed. McAllister told him to go to hell. The man swore that he would have the law on them. McAllister walked away and met the doctor hurrying through the gateway. He was a fiery little man in a hard hat and got to work without any fuss.

There were heads all around the corral wall now as the people gathered to stare. Kids climbed astride the wall and shouted: "Bang! Bang! You're dead." People started to push inside the gate and some even went up to the dead man and stared down at him ghoulishly, pointing to the blood and exclaiming. McAllister sent one of them to fetch the undertaker. He then went to the doctor who had finished with Holtz and was now tending the fellow with the bullet in his shoulder and asked how the wounded were. The doctor snapped that they'd all live and got on with his work. Next McAllister asked a bystander where criminals were locked up and was told that Bright put them in his store room.

McAllister gathered his men together and herded the prisoners along Fremont to the store. Here he was greeted by a distraught Mrs. Bright who wanted to know where her husband was. McAllister told her that he had been hurt, but assured her that he would be all right and should reach town soon. From her he obtained the key to the storeroom and locked the prisoners inside. He left Pete and Ruiz on guard there and went with Henry to the hotel on Main and booked a room. He left Holtz, white-faced, on the bed and went in search of the local justice. He kept his eyes skinned all the time for Church. He knew that at any second the challenge would come and he would be drawing his gun for his life. It was many years since he had been in a similar situation and it came as new to him. His nerves were as tight as a man who has never drawn a gun before.

At ten o'clock in the morning, after he had arranged for the trial of the prisoners, now supplemented by the wounded men, he was in the hotel room cleaning his gun. A clamor from the street took him to the window and he saw that the wagon had come in from the bench, bringing with it the wounded and more prisoners. Bright was there being greeted by his anxious wife.

McAllister holstered his gun and hurried down into the street to talk with Bright. By the time he reached him, the sheriff was sitting in his own parlor over the store and had a large whiskey in his hand. He greeted McAllister cheerfully and McAllister told him everything that had happened from his reaching Rigden's place to the fight at the corral.

Bright said, when he had finished: "It's all over, I reckon."

"Except for Church."

"We've a posse in town for that," Bright said.

"He's waited for me," McAllister said. "And it's me he's goin' to get. This is personal."

"Is he alone?"

"Not if I knew Joe. He'll want me to think he's alone and he'll tell everybody he is, but there'll be another gun up a side alley. A man can't change his habits when it comes to gun-fightin'."

"You watch out for yourself, Rem."

One other interesting thing happened before McAllister left the store. Bright said: "Before you go, I have a little present for you. Milly, take that gun out of the bureau yonder."

Mrs. Bright went to the old bureau, opened a drawer and brought out a hand-gun. McAllister took it and had a look at it. He had seen one like it before. It was a Le Mat, a French gun. It was a monster of a gun and he chuckled to see it. It had two barrels. It was of .40 caliber and had a single action. It held nine shots in its chambers and the second barrel, underneath the first, was a smooth-bore .66 caliber shotgun.

Bright said: "You clear the decks with buckshot and then pick off the remains with the nine shots."

McAllister chuckled.

"Bright," he said, "I'm surprised at you. I thought you were a peace-lovin' storekeeper."

Bright smiled.

"You're the only deputy I ever had," he said. "I don't want to lose you."

McAllister bade the two of them farewell and walked down through the store to the prison. Pete and Ruiz had had their places taken by some possemen now and were sleeping at the hotel. McAllister checked the prisoners were all right and went to the hotel himself. He washed himself and had a shave, not liking the idea of getting killed looking just anyhow. Then he lay down on a bed and fell into a dreamless sleep. He was awoken by Pete. A boy had come and left a message. Joe Church was getting impatient. Let McAllister come out on the street and settle it.

19

McALLISTER washed his face at the bowl. The others sat on their beds and watched him.

"You want we should take a hand, boss?" Pete asked.

"No, you keep outa this."

He buckled on his gun-belt and thrust the Le Mat into the waistband of his pants. He had carefully cleaned and oiled both guns.

Holtz said: "That Church is a polecat. Let one of us side you, Rem."

McAllister said: "I can handle Church. I'll see you fellows." He walked out of the room and down the stairs to the street. There was a flurry of movement to his right and he saw a buggy had entered town with two women in it. On either side were riders. McAllister picked out Rigden and his son Burt. Then he saw that the women were Rose and her sister. Willy Toff and Strange were there. He knew that their presence in town could mean only one thing. He went back into the hotel to his room, picked up the saddlebags with the money in them and went down to the street again. The buggy was now halted outside.

Rose was watching him, smiling wanly. He smiled back and touched his hat.

From the saddle, Rigden said: "My boy died, McAllister."

McAllister stepped forward and threw the saddlebags over the horn of the saddle. "There's your money."

"You got Gafferty?" McAllister nodded and matter-of-factly Rigden said: "I'm goin' to kill him."

"No," McAllister said, "you ain't goin' to do anything. I have Gafferty and he stands trial. You're all washed up in this territory, Rigden. Move on."

"Nobody talks to me that way." Some of the bite had gone out of his voice.

"I'm doin' it. You're finished. Get out while you can. The settlers don't love you too well after what you've done and I can't guarantee you protection."

Rigden laid his hand on his gun.

"I have all the protection I want here."

"A belt-gun ain't goin' to stop a bushwhacker. Mrs. Rigden, if he won't listen to me, perhaps you can talk some sense into his head." She shrugged her shoulders and looked away. Her favorite son was dead. Life held no more interest for her.

Rose started down from the buggy and McAllister offered her a hand.

"Rose," he said, "get off the street and stay off."

She looked up into his face and asked: "Is there going to be more trouble?" He nodded. "I don't have to tell you to be careful."

"You know me." He turned to

Rigden and said: "Get the ladies off the street, Rigden. There's going to be gun-play."

Wordlessly, Rigden got down from his horse and led the way into the hotel. His son Burt and the women followed him.

Willy Toff stepped into the buggy and said: "I hope you get your comeuppance."

"Willy," McAllister told him levelly, "if you're in town tomorrow, I'll arrest you. And that goes for you too, Strange."

Willy said: "You threatening me?"

McAllister said: "Yes." Willy looked at him for a moment, then slapped the backs of the horses with the lines and curved away across the street. Strange picked up the lines of the two saddle-horses and followed him.

McAllister watched them go.

It was an hour from dusk now and the light was no longer at its best. Not a time a gunfighter liked. He wondered what he should do — wait for Joe Church to come for him or to go looking for him.

Traffic was light at the moment, there were few people about. He regretted that lead, more lead, would have to be thrown in town. Sooner or later a bystander always got hurt.

There was a man standing motionless down toward Fremont who looked vaguely like Church. He was leaning on the sidewalk, building a smoke. McAllister was almost decided that this was Church when a shout from the other direction turned his head.

A man was walking down the center of the street.

This was Church.

There was no mistaking the tall lean frame, the loping slow walk. Something inside McAllister tightened until it was like a physical pain inside him. Then as suddenly as it came, it went and he was calm. He wiped the palm of his right hand on the leg of his pants. So this was it.

He noted that the sun was behind

Church. It was steeply angled and would be shining right in McAllister's eyes if he stepped out onto the street.

Somebody came out of the hotel behind him and stood near him. He turned his head and saw that it was Pete with a carbine in his hand.

"I'm watching the shadows, boss," the Indian said.

"Keep outa this."

"You can't make me, I reckon."

A man walked out of the hotel and crossed the street to the other side. He leaned against an upright of the sidewalk cover and started building a smoke. It was Ruiz.

"Where's Holtz?" McAllister asked sarcastically. "Ain't he in on this?"

"Up at the window with a greener."

Something warm flowed through McAllister. He didn't know his men thought so well of him. He wondered if Rose would be at the window watching and hoped not.

He realized that the street was almost empty.

Loosening the Remington in the leather, he stepped down from the sidewalk and paced slowly to the center of the street. He thought: *Joe likes to come close. He ain't goin' to get near me.* He'd like him come to within forty paces and then he'd cut him down. McAllister liked a long range and he knew his gun and what it could do.

Sixty paces.

There was silence near at hand. Only the distant sounds of the town continued. Somewhere a blacksmith sent out the music of his hammer on the anvil, a dog barked.

McAllister wondered where Church's hole card was. His eyes flicked along the street to the right and saw the shadowed maw of an alleyway. In the shadows he thought he caught a glimpse of metal. He turned his eyes the other way and saw that there was a second alleyway opposite the first. He lifted his eyes when he saw nothing in the alley and ran his eyes along the windows under the false fronts of the buildings. One sash was raised a foot with a corner of curtain fluttering and suddenly the curtain went still as though it had been pulled by a hand. It would be like Joe to have a man on either side of him. McAllister couldn't make out the mentality of the man. Why didn't he just gun him down from behind and have done with it?

Fifty paces.

A little too far even for a lover of distance like McAllister. Come a little closer Joe.

Somebody cocked a gun on the sidewalk and he guessed that was Pete.

McAllister could see the details of Joe Church's face now, every grim and tense line of it. He paced on evenly and McAllister knew that Joe was the calmer of the two. He had done this many times before. There had been other men in the shadows, but the set-up had been the same.

Forty-five paces.

Church called: "I'm goin' to kill you, Rem."

McAllister forced the stiffened muscles of his face into a grin.

"You're not goin' to get close enough, Joe."

Church broke his stride for a fraction of a second and in that moment there came to McAllister a remark of his old man. *The whole point of fighting is to stay alive. If you can't hit him, see he don't hit you.* That meant a gunfighter had to be quick as a dancer on his feet if he wanted to survive. And there were going to be four guns drawn against him. He didn't want speed, he wanted a miracle. He hoped to heaven that his men had the other enemy taped.

Forty paces.

Twice the distance that Joe liked. Now was the time to draw and try the long shot. It would have to be fast and sure before the men in the shadows could cut down on him.

His right hand jerked up, his little finger caught the inside curve of the butt and the gun came free into the palm of his hand. As the gun came up to the full extent of his arm, his thumb pulled the hammer back, the man came onto the foresight and he fired. As soon as the hammer hit, he flung himself to the right and down.

All hell broke loose.

Joe Church stumbled suddenly in his walk as though he had come unexpectedly on broken ground. A look of intense surprise showed on his face. He fell back a pace and his hand slapped down on the butt of his gun.

It seemed that in the same moment that McAllister fired, guns cut loose all along the street. Muzzle-flame and gunsmoke showed everywhere there was a dark shadow.

A window collapsed with a crash and tinkle of glass.

Pete yelled a wild war-cry and hit the boards of the sidewalk, firing as he landed. From above there came the boom of a scattergun as Holtz got to work.

Church was down now, firing as he lay in the dust.

Something struck McAllister's heel hard and it felt as though the whole foot had been torn off. He rested his arm on the ground and concentrated his whole attention on Church. He fired three steady shots and saw the man's head fall forward into the dust.

Then McAllister rolled to the right and kept on rolling until he was almost up against the side walk. Pete's gun boomed from above him.

McAllister fired at the alleyway opposite and then his gun was empty. He dropped it and rolled over to pull the Le Mat from his waistband. A bullet ripped into the sidewalk above him and he drove to his feet, running past Pete, heading for the nearest alleyway from which a man was firing on Ruiz on the far side of the street. As soon as he had covered a half-dozen yards he raised the Le Mat and let go with the lower barrel. A scream came from the alleyway. McAllister turned and faced the building opposite. He could see nothing more than the hand and gun of the man in the window firing down at Pete. He fired twice with the Le Mat.

The gun and hand that held it stayed where it was as the glass of the window crashed in. Through the gaping hole in the glass appeared the head and shoulders of a man. The hand released the gun. It clattered onto the roof of the sidewalk, rolled and fell to the ground. The man leaned on the sash and stayed there.

Gunsmoke drifted across the street. There was a stunned silence.

From his window, with smoking greener in his hands, Holtz called out: "That's it, boys."

McAllister's legs went suddenly weak under him and he thought he would fall down. Pete and Ruiz were walking toward him. The Mexican was shot in his gun arm, he held it with his left hand, but he was grinning.

Pete said: "I think your old friend Joe Church first-rate polecat. Better dead."

McAllister said: "Yeah — better

dead." Black depression descended on him. He looked at Church lying still on his face, the man who had once been his friend. A man took a wrong trail and a friendship was ended, a man died. But maybe Joe hadn't died here on this street, he had died years back when he had taken that other trail. Violent death was the only way out for him.

Somebody called his name.

He looked up and saw Rose standing on the sidewalk outside the hotel. There were people all around her, but he saw only her. She was the answer, she was the peace that he sought. He put the Le Mat away under his belt and walked toward her.

She ran down from the sidewalk and came into his arms.

"You see, honey," he told her, "I was careful like you said."

Books by Matt Chisholm
in the Linford Western Library:

HARD TEXAS TRAIL

McALLISTER ON THE COMANCHE CROSSING

McALLISTER AND THE SPANISH GOLD

McALLISTER NEVER SURRENDERS

McALLISTER DIE-HARD

McALLISTER AND CHEYENNE DEATH

McALLISTER — QUARRY

McALLISTER FIRE-BRAND

RAGE OF McALLISTER

THE TRAIL OF FEAR

McALLISTER — WOLF-BAIT

A BULLET FOR BRODY

McALLISTER MAKES WAR

GUN LUST

STAMPEDE

McALLISTER'S FURY

HUNTED
SPUR TO DEATH
CASH McCORD

Other titles in the Linford Western Library:

TOP HAND
Wade Everett

The Broken T was big. But no ranch is big enough to let a man hide from himself.

GUN WOLVES OF LOBO BASIN
Lee Floren

The Feud was a blood debt. When Smoke Talbot found the outlaws who gunned down his folks he aimed to nail their hide to the barn door.

SHOTGUN SHARKEY
Marshall Grover

The westbound coach carrying the indomitable Larry and Stretch headed for a shooting showdown.

FIGHTING RAMROD
Charles N. Heckelmann

Most men would have cut their losses, but Frazer counted the bullets in his guns and said he'd soak the range in blood before he'd give up another inch of what was his.

LONE GUN
Eric Allen

Smoke Blackbird had been away too long. The Lequires had seized the Blackbird farm, forcing the Indians and settlers off, and no one seemed willing to fight! He had to fight alone.

THE THIRD RIDER
Barry Cord

Mel Rawlins wasn't going to let anything stand in his way. His father was murdered, his two brothers gone. Now Mel rode for vengeance.